"Is this not an ingenio[...] said as they strolled about the edges of the stage. "I have yet to see an opera here, and so it is my first visit. What a fabulously beautiful place this is!"

"I suppose so. I never really noticed." He wasn't noticing now, either, for he was captivated by the way she hungrily drank in every detail, eyes and cheeks glowing.

"Oh, how could you not? Only look at the painted ceiling and the crystal chandeliers. It is almost like a French chateau. How I would love to see an opera here someday."

"Is that on your list, too?"

She laughed and slapped him playfully on the arm. "Of course it is. But tonight is an altogether different sort of treat. All of these spectacular costumes and laughter and music," she said and spread her arms wide. "Is it not marvelous?"

Her face flushed so sweetly in her excitement, Max could not resist touching it. He ran a finger against a cheek. It was as soft and warm as he'd expected. "Very clever," he said. She gave a bit of a start at his touch and so he backed off. He ought to leave now before he did something truly stupid. Rosalind was an innocent, not one of his worldly widows. He must keep reminding himself that she was not for him. . . .

Miss Lacey's Last Fling

Candice Hern

A SIGNET BOOK

SIGNET
Published by New American Library, a division of
Penguin Putnam Inc., 375 Hudson Street,
New York, New York 10014, U.S.A.
Penguin Books Ltd, 27 Wrights Lane,
London W8 5TZ, England
Penguin Books Australia Ltd, Ringwood,
Victoria, Australia
Penguin Books Canada Ltd, 10 Alcorn Avenue,
Toronto, Ontario, Canada M4V 3B2
Penguin Books (N.Z.) Ltd, 182–190 Wairau Road,
Auckland 10, New Zealand

Penguin Books Ltd, Registered Offices:
Harmondsworth, Middlesex, England

First published by Signet, an imprint of New American Library,
a division of Penguin Putnam Inc.

First Printing, February 2001
10 9 8 7 6 5 4 3 2 1

To Hilary Ross,
the world's most patient editor

Chapter 1

"What are all those trunks and bandboxes doing in the front hall? What is happening?"

Ursula, Lady Walgrave, swept into the library in the regal way she had adopted since marrying Lord Geoffrey Walgrave. She came to a halt in the middle of the room, stabbed the point of her parasol into the thick Turkish carpet, and glared down at her father. Sir Edmund Lacey sat behind the big oak desk looking thoroughly bewildered at the mountain of papers and ledgers before him, unmoved by his daughter's grand entrance.

"Well?" Ursula prompted. She kept one kid-gloved finger on the knob handle of her parasol, not quite leaning onto it like a walking stick, but rather striking an elegant pose.

Sir Edmund looked up and blinked. "Eh? What's that?"

Ursula sighed theatrically. "The baggage, Papa. In the front hall. Whose is it?"

"Oh. I suppose it must be Rosie's."

"Rosie's?"

Ursula appeared to notice her eldest sister for the first time. Rosalind Lacey stood in the corner of the room, near the window, where the morning sun poured in thick and bright directly upon her, illuminating the brown velvet of her pelisse so that it shone like polished bronze. She did not believe for one minute that Ursula had not known she was there. Since her elevation to the wife of a local baron three years earlier, however, Lady Walgrave gave little notice to her spinster sister. Except, of course, when Rosie was needed—to help nurse a sick child, or to help write out invitations in her elegant hand, or to even out the numbers whenever an extra female was needed at the last moment.

Ursula eyed Rosie up and down, taking in her traveling clothes with disapproval. Whether her sister objected to the fact that she was dressed for travel, or simply to the unfashionable cut of her pelisse, Rosie could not have said. "I do not understand," Ursula said. "Surely, you are not going anywhere."

Rosie smiled at her sister's confident tone and was about to respond when Papa spoke up.

"She's going to London," he said in the same tone of utter disbelief he had been using since Rosie had shown him Aunt Fanny's letter.

"She's not," Ursula said. "She can't be." She stared at Rosie. "You can't be."

Rosie smiled. "I am," she said.

"But . . . but that is ridiculous," Ursula said. "Why on earth would you be going to London? There is nothing for you in town. I cannot imagine what you must be thinking. You've never needed to go before, when Pamela and I— Oh. Oh, no. Do not tell me you are going for the Season?"

"Well, I suppose the Season will be in full swing when I arrive," Rosie said, "so I daresay I shall be there for it."

"But you cannot! Papa, tell her she cannot."

"I see no reason to do so," Sir Edmund said. "I confess, the announcement has surprised me as much as you, Ursula, but I do not know why Rosie should not be allowed to go. She is old enough to do as she pleases." His diffident tone lacked the conviction of his words. He ran agitated fingers through his thick, gray hair, heedless of the tousled disarray he created.

Sir Edmund had been thoroughly abashed by Rosie's announcement that she was going to London. Nevertheless, he never once suggested she should not go, bless his heart.

"That is just the problem," Ursula said. "She is *too* old." She turned and cast her disdainful glance upon Rosie once again. "Surely you do not mean to try your luck at the Marriage Mart. Not at your age. You will only succeed in making yourself, and your family, look ridiculous. We shall be the laughingstock of the *ton*. I am sure Walgrave would be most displeased."

Rosie had long ago suppressed the persistent desire to pinch her sister's head off. Of all the family, Ursula had always been the one most concerned with appearances, with propriety, with rank and form and proper behavior. Before she had left the schoolroom, she had been able to recite without error the entire female order of precedence, from Queen all the way down to wife of a burgess. Though she had never dared say so in front of their father, Ursula's siblings had been made to understand the unfortunate circumstance of being the children of no greater personage than a minor baronet.

Rosie was not the only member of the family who had breathed a sigh of relief when Ursula had managed to bring Lord Walgrave up to scratch.

But even Ursula's sharp tongue would not deter Rosie from her purpose. She was going to London, and she could think of nothing at the moment that would be allowed to stop her.

"Have no fear, Ursula," she said. "I have no intention of setting myself up to find a husband. I am more aware than you might imagine of the pointlessness of such an endeavor."

"Then there is no need for you to leave at all," Ursula said, "is there?"

"To be sure, there is no *need*. But there is desire. I wish to go, that is all. A bit of a holiday, if you will."

Ursula clicked her tongue and tapped her toe impatiently. "How utterly ridiculous," she said. "I repeat, there is nothing for you in town, my dear."

"Perhaps," Rosie said. "But I wish to go, nevertheless. I'd like to go to the opera and the galleries and the Tower and—oh, so many things. With you and Pamela married and Thomas finished at university and the twins away at Harrow, there is only Papa to look after. And with you so nearby, he should be fine. He has agreed—have you not, Papa?—to struggle along without me for a while."

"So I have," he said, a tentative smile touching his lips. "And a struggle it shall be, I assure you. I confess I had not realized how much you do for us here at Wycombe, my dear. Indeed, I feel quite ashamed that I have so neglected my own duties and left them to you." He closed the ledger he'd been studying and rose from his chair behind the desk. "Yes, Ursula, Rosie shall have her holiday, and well deserved it will be. I set aside money for each of you girls to have a Season in town. But after your mother died"—he paused and sighed wistfully as he always did when he spoke of his late wife—"Rosie took on so many of her duties that we could never seem to spare her. And, I am ashamed to admit, it never even occurred to me that she might want a Season." He shook his head and clucked his tongue. "We have been horribly unfair to your sister, Ursula. Of course she shall have her Season in town, late though it may be."

He walked around the desk and over to the corner where Rosie stood, and took both her hands in his. "And if you happen to come home with a handsome young lord on your arm who wishes to be your husband, then he shall be welcome, my dear. I do not know what your sister can be thinking, but you are not too old to find a husband. You are only four and twenty, after all."

"Six and twenty," Rosie said.

"Really?" Sir Edmund looked at her quizzically. "Good heavens, how time has slipped away from me. Even so, you are not too old. And you are very pretty, my dear. So like your mother."

"Papa." This was not a topic Rosie wished to pursue. She did indeed strongly resemble her mother, and her father had always thought his wife the most beautiful woman in the world. But Sir Edmund had gazed upon his wife with eyes blinded by love. She had not in fact been a beauty. At best, she would have been considered handsome. And Rosie had inherited her thick brown hair, her long nose, her deep-set hazel eyes, her wide mouth, and her tall, angular figure. Rosie was no beauty.

"Yes, my dear," her father was saying, "you are pretty enough to draw any man's attention. Perhaps you will upstage your sister and bring home a duke, eh?"

"Papa!" Rosie smiled at Sir Edmund's outrageous suggestion. "I have no intention of bringing home a duke, or any other man, for that matter. I have told you, I am not interested in finding a husband." It was too late for that, though not for the reasons Ursula or Sir Edmund may have thought.

"Then I really see no reason for you to leave Wycombe," Ursula said. "I have my own family to look after and can spare little time to oversee matters here. Besides, I cannot imagine you would find London to your liking at all, Rosie. You will either be bored or scandalized. You are much too prim and straight-laced for high society."

Rosie bit back a smile as she considered how she

planned to burst out of those tight laces once she got to London. Before it was too late.

"And where did you plan to stay?" Ursula continued. "I had not heard that Lady Hartwell planned a trip to town, as she did with both Pamela and me. Who would act as your chaperone?"

"I will be staying with Aunt Fanny," Rosie said, and steeled herself for the outburst that would surely follow.

"What!" Ursula's face grew dangerously crimson. "You cannot mean it. Aunt Fanny! Papa, say it is not so."

"I'm afraid it is so," Sir Edmund replied and walked over to the desk and rifled through the pile of papers until he located his sister's letter. "See here. She has written to invite Rosie to stay for a few months."

This was too much for Ursula, and she finally dropped her elegant pose and sank into the nearest chair. "Aunt Fanny," she said, shaking her head in disbelief. "We are doomed."

Their father's older sister was the black sheep of his conservative family, having demonstrated a wild streak in her youth which had not abated, even as she settled into her senior years. She had been the subject of gossip for decades, and had grown rather notorious for her parties, her gambling, and most of all for her string of lovers. It was even said that she had once had a brief affair with the Prince of Wales, somewhere between his alliances with Mrs. Fitzherbert and Lady Jersey. Rosie could think of no one more appropriate to help her loosen those tight laces that had bound her for so long.

Aunt Fanny, otherwise known as Lady Parkhurst, had visited Wycombe Hall two or three times over the years—brief stops on her way to some infamous house party or other. She would sweep in with her French gowns and stylish hats and haughty manner, oblivious to the fact that she was never invited and not made especially welcome by Sir Edmund. His obvious disapproval made no difference to Aunt Fanny. As children, they had all been wide-eyed with fascination each time their aunt made an appearance. As they got older and better understood the stories about her, most of them found her behavior shocking and wanted nothing to do with her.

Though she still felt a trifle skittish at the prospect of meeting Aunt Fanny again, Rosie secretly admired her, not so much for any of the wild things she was rumored to have done, but for having the courage to live her life exactly as she pleased.

And now Rosie, too, wanted to do as she pleased. Oh, nothing so shocking or improper as Aunt Fanny's escapades. Rosie's desires were simpler, not so daring. Even so, she needed to gain courage to do them, and who better to teach her such courage than Aunt Fanny? Assuming her resolution remained firm and she did not crumple at the formidable woman's feet.

But Rosie had no fear of losing her resolve. It was now or never.

"We are doomed," Ursula repeated. "If Rosie goes about with Aunt Fanny, heaven only knows what sort of scrape she may fall into."

"I am not a child, Ursula."

Ursula gave her a condescending look. "Not in years, certainly. But I am a married woman and know more about these things. You are an innocent, Rosie, and may easily be led into all sorts of folly. Your reputation may be ruined completely. Oh, Papa! How could you countenance such a thing? The woman may be your sister, but you know what she is. Dear Lord, we shall none of us be able to show our faces in town again."

Rosie laughed. "I don't think it is so bad as that," she said.

"Yes, it is," Ursula said. "Aunt Fanny, for God's sake. We are doomed."

"And now we embark upon yet another Season." Maxwell Davenant sank back languidly against the soft cushions of the settee and expelled a sigh of pure ennui. "What a bore."

"An uninspiring prospect, indeed," his hostess said. "All those balls and routs and card parties and such. Nothing of the least interest to keep a person occupied."

Max slanted a glance toward Frances, Lady Parkhurst, to find a smug grin on her face. "You mock me, madam."

"How can I not," she said, "when you insist on making such foolish remarks? Boredom, indeed!"

But Max was, in fact, bored. He was thirty-six and this would be his eighteenth Season—half his life spent doing the same thing year after year. This year would be no different from the year before or the year before that. Or from the next year.

If there was a next year.

His hand crept up to his waistcoat pocket and fingered the edge of parchment tucked within. Freddie had known what Max meant. Freddie had been bored, had said precisely that in his suicide note. Throughout the year since his friend's death, Max had come to the conclusion that Freddie Moresby had had the right of it: make an exit at his own time, before ennui and age slowly sucked the life out of him.

"Surely you do not find the same old rounds thrilling from year to year, Fanny?" he asked. "After all, you're—" He paused before he said something he should not.

"I'm what?" she asked. "So old I can remember more Seasons than Methuselah? Well, so I can, but I do not recall ever being bored. Since Basil died, of course, nothing has been quite as enjoyable to me as it once was." She sighed dramatically and placed a hand upon her cheek. "But I go on."

"You do, indeed," Max said, unaffected by her feigned melancholy. Though only a scant year or two in front of seventy, Fanny Parkhurst was still a vibrant and attractive woman. She'd been his father's mistress and he a callow youth when they'd first met, and they had remained friends ever since. He spent many an evening in her drawing room, which was often filled with a diverse and lively assortment of wits and beaux. During the afternoons, however, she was at home to no one but himself and a few others.

"I trust Lord Eldridge," he said, referring to Fanny's latest cicisbeo, "does not bore you, my dear?"

"He does not, you impudent puppy, as if it were any of your business. Nevertheless, I suspect I shall indeed find this Season horribly pedestrian. Did I not tell you that my niece is coming to town?"

"Your niece? Good Lord, Fanny, do not tell me you are to be the girl's chaperone?"

"Apparently so."

Max gave a crack of laughter. "Oh, surely not, Fanny. No one could seriously imagine you in the role of bear-leader. Ha! It is too ridiculous." He laughed at her look of mock outrage, but soon enough, her own laughter joined his. Fanny, better than anyone, would appreciate the sheer absurdity of Lady Parkhurst as chaperone to any respectable young lady.

"Stop laughing, you horrid boy," she said. "It is not a source of amusement for me, I assure you. I certainly have no wish to play chaperone to anyone, but most especially not to this young woman."

"Oh?" Max's interest was piqued. "And why not? Who is she?"

"Rosalind Lacey, the eldest daughter of my younger brother, Edmund."

"Sir Edmund Lacey? The one you always called the driest limb on the family tree?"

"The very one," Fanny said. "A duller, more tedious man I have seldom met. And yet somehow that dry old stick managed to sprout several new twigs. Six children! Three girls, three boys. Why is it that all the dull ones manage to procreate so easily?"

Max did not comment. Fanny had had only one child of her own—he discounted the old rumors of a by-blow from an earlier alliance, or even a half-sibling from her many years with his own father—and that child had contracted influenza during his last term at Oxford and died shortly afterward. How it must gall Fanny to know that her own wit and liveliness would not live on in another, while her tiresome brother had managed to produce six insipid offspring.

"Of course," she said, "his poor wife died many years back, leaving him alone with all those children." She shuddered visibly.

"And so now Sir Edmund will start sending his wretched motherless girls to you," Max said, "so that you may launch them into Society?"

"Well now, that is one of the curious things about this whole business," she said. "The two younger girls have already been fired off and married. Came to town in their own time and avoided me like the pox, for which, frankly, I was quite thankful. Led about by some Devonshire neighbor, the respectable Lady Something-or-other. But now it's the eldest girl, the most irksome of the lot, who is coming to stay. And Edmund did not ask me to take her. Goodness, he hasn't written three words to me in years. No, it was Rosalind herself who wrote, asking if she might visit."

"And charitable soul that you are," Max said, "you found it difficult to refuse such a direct request, no doubt."

"Well, what was I to do?" Fanny gave a decidedly Gallic shrug. "The troublesome creature appealed to my worst instincts. She actually said she wanted to, and I quote, 'experience all that London has to offer.' She could think of no better guide to the most amusing entertainments than her dear Aunt Fanny."

"Clever girl."

"On the contrary, my boy. Rosalind is a priggish, docile little creature so totally lacking in spirit that even to picture her at one the entertainments you and I might enjoy is simply beyond imagining. Of all Edmund's brood, this one always seemed meek as a governess—quietly managing the lives of her siblings after their mother's death while keeping herself in the background."

"She sounds a veritable mouse," Max said.

"And so she is. Good heavens, Max, what am I to do with such an odious girl?"

He put up his hands in a defensive gesture. "Don't cast your eyes in my direction, Fanny. Leave me out of it, I beg you. I have no taste for the prim governess type, as you well know."

"But darling, you must not desert me in my time of need. If I am to parade this chit about town, all my other friends will surely abandon me. I am counting on your support."

Max leaned forward in his chair, tapping his quizzing glass against his knee. "If you expect me to squire the mouse around and dance with her at balls, then you are out, Fanny, for I won't do it."

Fanny brushed aside his concern with a dismissive wave of her hand. "I would never ask such a frightful thing of you, Max. Besides, my objective is to attach the girl to some dull, unsuspecting swain as soon as possible and get her off my hands. I have no doubt she is coming to town in search of one of those stolid, respectable husbands one hears so much about but seldom meets. Good Lord, how am I to find such a paragon?"

Max arched a brow. "Not to put too fine a point on it, my dear," he said, "but aren't you afraid your own notorious career along with my scandalous presence might have the effect of scaring off the very sort you wish to attract?"

"What a horrid boy you are, Max. But have no fear. I don't expect you to court the poor creature. I merely hoped to count on your company from time to time when I must take her about town with me. And perhaps to restrain me from flinging her into the Thames when she becomes particularly tiresome."

"What a bore."

"Indeed."

Chapter 2

"**O**h, miss, what be that awful smell?"

Rosie tore her gaze from out the carriage window to look at her maid, who sat on the opposite bench, nose twitching like a bunny. "I believe it is just the smell of the city, Violet. See how the air is slightly smoky? We're not in the country anymore."

"Lord help us," Violet said.

The maid's misgivings were not unwarranted. They had entered London some miles back and so far it was not quite what Rosie had expected. The Metropolis was big and crowded, as she had known it would be. But neither of her sisters—both of whom had been rapturous about their Seasons in town—had mentioned anything like the areas of squalor they were now passing through. Old, ramshackle buildings with grime-darkened windows—or no windows at all—lined the narrow, dark alleys and courts that led off the main street. Dingy doorways teemed with filthy urchins, dour laborers, exhausted slatterns, and sprawling drunkards.

"Are you sure 'bout this, Miss Lacey? Coachman'll turn right back 'round to Wycombe Hall, if'n ye asked."

Rosie smiled at the young girl's look of disgust. "Yes, Violet, I am quite sure of what I'm doing."

She became even more confident as the scenery abruptly changed to broad streets lined with large, new, fine-looking buildings. Tidy, bow-windowed shop fronts faced the street, which was flanked on each side by elevated pavements of clean, bright flagstone crowded with fashionably dressed men and women. Boys swept the pavement with rush brooms and were offered coins by gentlemen strollers. Street corners were the territories of hawkers shouting the day's news and ballad singers singing their tales. Three-Penny Postmen darted through the crowds, ringing their bells as they passed.

Suddenly, it all seemed very exciting.

"You see, Violet?" Rosie said. "It is not so bad as you thought."

The maid wrinkled her nose. "I still say it smells funny."

"One comes to London for the Society and the art and the culture, not the fresh air and scenery," Rosie said. "We can have that back in Devon."

"Ay, and ye'll be missin' it soon enough, I declare."

"It will all be there when we return," Rosie said. "But I cannot see the opera in Devon. Nor visit art galleries, nor watch a play in a real theater, nor see the menagerie at the Tower, nor attend grand balls, nor all sorts of other things I've come to London to do."

Violet gave an indiscreet snort. "Whatever ye says, miss."

Amused by Violet's rustic apprehensions, Rosie had no intention of allowing her own niggling fears to interfere with her plans.

When the headaches had first begun, she had been afraid she may have contracted the same mysterious illness that had killed her mother. After the diagnosis had been confirmed—by an Exeter physician she had secretly consulted—she had been almost paralyzed with fear. But then she took stock of her life and uncovered an enormous ache in her soul for all she did not know and would never know, for all she had not done and would never do.

Rosie had succumbed to overwhelming waves of self-pity at first, lamenting the waste of so many years looking after others, allowing her own life to pass by in uneventful routine. But it was not too late, not yet, to take back her life before disease incapacitated her.

She had no doubt that London and Aunt Fanny would be the best medicine of all.

"Lord, bless me, what is that place, miss?"

Rosie looked out the carriage window to see an odd-looking building, its ornate Egyptian facade a sharp contrast to the simple buildings on either side. A small crowd of people were queued up outside the entrance. "Oh, that must be the Egyptian Exhibition Hall," she said. "I read about it in one of the guide books. Mr. Bullock offers exhibits of all sorts of things. In fact, I believe he recently exhibited Napoleon's carriage. Perhaps it is still on display."

"Ooh, do ye think so, miss?"

"We shall have to find out. Then we'll come have a look, shall we?"

"Oh, yes, miss. I should like to see that. Thank you, miss."

Rosie smiled at her maid's sudden change of heart. She reached for her reticule and pulled out a flat ivory case from which she extracted a small notebook and tiny ivory-handled pencil. She flipped to a half-filled page and added a note.

Visit Egyptian Hall.

The list was growing.

Rosie hung on to the strap as their coach made its laborious way through such traffic as she could never have imagined. Donkey carts piled with produce, brewers' carts and coal wagons pulled by enormous draft horses, elegant calashes, plain black hackney coaches, post chaises, curricles, and mail coaches—all filled the

broad streets so that it became almost impossible to
pass. Barreling through it all at reckless speed came
a sporting vehicle so sleek and compact the driver
must feel as if he were flying. Oh, how she would
love to ride in one of those. She scribbled another
note.

Ride in a sporting vehicle.

Or, better yet:

Drive a sporting vehicle. Why not?

Their coach came to yet another abrupt halt and
Rosie peeked out the window to see a sedan chair
carried along by two stout young men. Inside, she
caught the briefest glimpse of an elegantly coifed
woman whose face was obscured by a large fan. Nat-
tily attired men who strolled along the pavement
craned their necks to get a look at the woman, some
doffing their hats. Smartly dressed women turned
away.

Who could she be? A member of the demimonde?
It must make her feel like a queen to be carried around
like that.

Rosie moistened the tip of her pencil with her
tongue, pleased, though somewhat overwhelmed, at
the growing size of her list.

Ride in a sedan chair.

Heavens, there was so much to do. And so little
time. To be perfectly truthful, she could not be sure
about the time, but it could not be more than six
months at best. Her mother, God rest her soul, had
not lasted even that long.

She tucked the notebook back in its case and returned it to her reticule. There was enough on the list
to keep her very busy for quite some time. The trick
would be to fill every hour of the day and not waste
a single moment.

Rosie was going to have a grand time in London.

*   *   *

Max had just settled himself comfortably in one of Fanny's lush armchairs when he heard the sounds of a carriage pulling up out front, followed by an extraordinary amount of bustling. Blast! After a long night of exquisite debauchery with a notorious widow, he had risen late in the day, overcome with the inexplicable ennui that had so plagued him of late. He had dragged himself to Fanny's in hopes she could cheer him out of his doldrums.

"Dammit, Fanny," he said, "I thought you weren't at home to visitors today. I had hoped not to have to put on my public face this afternoon. I really do not believe I am up to it." He uttered a groan and made a move to rise, but Fanny held up her hand to stop him.

"I am not receiving visitors, Max, so you may stay put. Quigley will send them away."

But the butler did no such thing. A few minutes later, footsteps sounded on the stairs and, after a perfunctory knock, Quigley opened the parlor doors.

"Miss Lacey has arrived, my lady."

Fanny cast Max a brief glance and rolled her eyes heavenward. Good Lord, it was the tiresome niece. He must make his exit. Max rose as a young woman was ushered into the room.

"My dear Rosalind," Fanny said, her voice so cheerful and welcoming that Max had to marvel at her instinctive graciousness. She had been grumbling about this loathsome responsibility for weeks. "Do come in and join me for a cup of tea while your maid sees to your bedchamber. Quigley?" She muttered quick instructions to the butler then took the girl's arm and led her into the parlor.

"You must be exhausted from your journey," Fanny continued. "I promise I won't keep you from your rest for long. But do sit down for a moment, won't you? Here, let me take your pelisse and gloves and bonnet."

Max watched from his corner while the girl allowed Fanny to take her in hand. She had not yet uttered a word and looked overwhelmed, if not precisely frightened, by her formidable aunt.

Max stifled a groan as the girl removed a plain bonnet to reveal dark brown hair pulled back into a tight, prim knot at the back of her neck. She looked every inch the mouse Fanny had described. Not a tiny mouse, however. She was taller than Fanny, though she hunched her shoulders inward, making her appear smaller. Beneath an unattractive brown pelisse, she wore a simple sprigged muslin dress that hung loosely on her lanky frame. Its pale yellow color made her skin look sallow.

Her face was unremarkable, save for rather large eyes of indeterminate color and good bone structure. Max was a connoisseur of beautiful women and could assess in a glance the potential of any female face. Much could be made of good eyes and good bones, but this girl had done nothing to make the best of those features.

And she was no girl, really. He would guess that she would never see twenty-five again.

Poor Fanny. What was she to do with such a dowd?

Miss Lacey shook out her wrinkled skirts and offered her aunt a wan smile. "Thank you, ma'am," she said in a voice that was both surprisingly confident and intriguingly husky.

It was at that moment, while Max pondered the rich tones of her voice, that the girl looked up and caught his eye. She held his gaze for a brief instant, then turned to her aunt, lifting her brows in question.

"Oh, how frightfully rude of me," Fanny exclaimed. "Max, darling, allow me to present to you my niece, Miss Lacey. Rosalind, this is Mr. Davenant."

Fanny's sudden lapse into propriety caused Max almost to burst out laughing. Mr. Davenant, indeed. Well, this chit held no such hold on his own behavior. Perhaps he would just see if he could make the mouse run.

He lifted his quizzing glass and eyed the girl through it, slowly studying her from head to foot. The survey revealed little or nothing to hold his attention. If the woman had any curves they were thoroughly masked by the too-large dress. When the glass reached her face again, she was staring back at him wide-eyed.

Out of sheer badness, Max decided to continue taunting the mouse. Swinging the glass on its ribbon, he languidly crossed the room and stood before her.

"Your servant, Miss Lacey," he said, then reached for her hand and brought it to his lips. He allowed his tongue to flicker briefly across her bare knuckles before lifting his head. Expecting outrage, Max was surprised to discover that despite a rather stiff-necked apprehension, amusement twinkled in the girl's eyes—they were hazel, after all—and a smile tugged at the corners of her lips. Perhaps she wasn't as much of a mouse as Fanny believed her to be.

And perhaps the Season would not be such a bore after all.

Rosie watched Mr. Davenant take his leave and then sat down on the settee indicated by her aunt. She absently rubbed at the knuckles that still tingled from the touch of his lips. And tongue! Good heavens, she had so much to learn.

"Who was that man, Aunt Fanny?"

"I told you, my dear, that was Mr. Davenant."

Rosie accepted the tea passed to her, took a restorative sip, and studied her aunt over the rim of the cup. Aunt Fanny was older than Papa but looked younger, with striking silver hair and bright, expressive blue eyes. "I recall his name, ma'am. But who *is* he? I mean, is he a friend of yours? Is he someone important? I've never been to London, you see, and am quite ignorant of Society. Should I have recognized his name?"

Her aunt placed her teacup down on the table and gave Rosie her full attention. "Max Davenant is the greatest rake in all of London. He is more notorious than . . . than I am." She gave a little lift to her chin, as though proclaiming pride in her own notoriety. Rosie thought perhaps the old woman was trying to shock her, but she was only intrigued. In fact, if she hadn't thought it would be terribly rude, she would have taken out her notebook and scribbled an addition to her list.

Flirt with a rake. Or perhaps:

Flirt with the greatest rake in all of London.

She wasn't altogether certain how to go about it, but she would learn. It had been her plan all along to kick up her heels a bit, to have fun while visiting Aunt Fanny. But after Ursula's outburst, Rosie had harbored a devilish desire to do something truly wild and outrageous, if only to annoy her smug sister. Meeting her first rake only whetted her appetite for adventure.

Rosie could not have said she had ever before encountered a rake, but she would have known Mr. Davenant for one even without her aunt's pointed reference. She supposed he might be thought handsome, with his dark eyes, firm jaw, and patrician nose. But she suspected his looks had little to do with his success with women. He had an air about him—a sort of sleepy-eyed negligence that, coupled with a languid grace, lent him an aura of . . . well, she could only call it seduction.

Rosie had felt the full force of his seductive manner, even in the few minutes he had been in the room. The wretched man had practically undressed her with his eyes, peering through that horrid quizzing glass. No one had ever looked at her in such a way, or made such a lascivious gesture out of kissing her hand.

Not so long ago, she supposed she would have slapped a man for treating her with such disrespect. More likely, she would have swooned. Now, she rather enjoyed the notion of a man flirting with her, especially a notorious rake. It was amazing how quickly one's attitudes could change. Max Davenant was just the sort of person she had hoped to meet in London, someone with whom she might scandalize her priggish sister. After all, what harm could a little scandal do when she would be gone in a few months?

"Is Mr. Davenant one of your lovers?" The words were out of her mouth even as the thought entered her mind. Rosie could hardly believe she had said such a thing, and hoped the heat in her cheeks did not translate into a visible blush.

Aunt Fanny arched a brow. "No," she said. Rosie's disappointment must her shown on her face, for her aunt smiled and said, "But his father was."

Rosie returned her aunt's smile, and for the first time felt truly at ease in the woman's presence. "I cannot thank you enough," she said, "for allowing me to visit you in London. I realize it is a bold imposition from someone you hardly know."

"Nonsense, my dear. You are most welcome. But I confess you are not at all what I expected. I believe you have grown up, Rosalind."

Rosie chuckled softly and considered that her fearsome aunt was not such a bad sort after all. "Because I am not shocked to know you have had lovers, you think I am grown up?" Rosie asked. "I assure you, Aunt Fanny, that though I have reached the ripe old age of six-and-twenty, I do not feel so very grown up. I haven't done much living, you see, and I have come to London to change that."

Her aunt's eyes widened. "You have come to town to—"

"To live. To go to interesting places and meet fascinating people and do all sorts of new things."

"And to find a husband, perhaps?"

"Good heavens, no! Is that what you thought? Well, I daresay that is what most people will think, but I tell you, aunt, that is the very last thing on my mind. In fact, I can tell you with absolute certainty that I will *not* be returning to Devon with a husband in tow. No, I can assure you that will not happen."

Aunt Fanny stared for a moment, then shook her head in disbelief. "You astonish me, Rosalind. I was sure that you would want—well, never mind that. So, am I to understand that you simply want to . . . to enjoy yourself?"

"Precisely. And I could think of no one better to show me how to do that."

Aunt Fanny threw back her head and laughed. "I should think not," she said, "for I suspect few have enjoyed life as much as I have. Well, my girl, you must tell me how we should begin. What would you like to do?"

"Oh, I have a list." Rosie patted her reticule, but was suddenly embarrassed to actually reveal the list to someone else. There were things on it she would rather not have anyone see. Like the note about being thoroughly kissed. Or the one yet to be added about flirting with rakes. "I've been jotting down things I'd like to do, but I can tell you what the very first thing is."

"Yes?"

"You told me I had grown up. Well, I want to feel grown up. Look at me." She spread her arms out to her sides. "My clothes are awful, my hair is too long. I'm tired of being such a drab."

Aunt Fanny's eyes narrowed as she took in Rosie's

appearance, though she was too polite to say anything.

"You see, aunt, I want to go to the opera and the theater and attend balls and routs and such. But I don't want to tag along looking like a country mouse."

She threw pride to the winds and gave her aunt a beseeching look. "You always look so fashionable," Rosie said, casting an admiring glance at Fanny's simple but stylish dress of striped Scotch jaconet muslin. "I was hoping you could recommend a good modiste and perhaps a hairdresser. Papa gave me quite a bit of money—because I never had a Season, you see—and I can think of no better way to spend it. Aunt Fanny, I want to be transformed."

Chapter 3

Aunt Fanny threw herself wholeheartedly into the business of turning Rosie into a pattern card of fashion. Rosie was quite sure her aunt was thoroughly enjoying herself.

"You have great potential, my dear," she had said. "We must do what we can to set you off to your best advantage. When we are through, I guarantee you will have all the gentlemen's heads turning."

"You forget, Aunt Fanny, that I am not in the market for a husband."

"Even so, a woman should never stop trying to turn heads."

She had gained her aunt's approval during their initial visit to Madame Dussault. When the modiste learned it was Rosie's first trip to London, she brought out muslins and sarcenets in pastel shades befitting a young woman making her debut into Society. Rosie had objected.

"I am neither young nor 'coming out,'" she said. "I am merely visiting my aunt and have no desire to dress as though I am just out of the schoolroom. I believe I should prefer more color. Like these, perhaps." She indicated a deep blue satin and an emerald green silk.

Once Madame Dussault had understood Rosie's requirements, and had received a discreet nod of approval from Aunt Fanny, she and her assistants entered into the business with enthusiasm. Except for an aversion to pastels, Rosie had little notion of what she wanted, or even what might look best. It had been years since she'd given much thought to her wardrobe. But the latest fashions, to her backward rustic sensibilities, looked fussy and overdone. She had a sinking notion that when Madame Dussault was through, she would look like some Bartholomew baby, when she had hoped to look sophisticated, worldly—like someone who could rightfully flirt with a notorious rake. Or two.

Without a word passing between them, Aunt Fanny seemed to understand exactly what Rosie wanted. She scoffed at the elaborate flounces, frills, and furbelows, and reminded Madame that her niece was no adolescent.

"Look at those bones, Madame," her aunt had said as she brushed a gloved finger along Rosie's jaw. "It would be criminal to obscure such refinement with overwrought decoration and excess ornament. Color, texture, line. That is what is important."

Rosie marveled at her aunt's innate sense of style, and sent up a silent prayer of thanks that she was to benefit from it. Fanny insisted that the auburn highlights in Rosie's brown hair would best be brought out with deep reds and coppers and mulberries, that her height should be emphasized with vertical lines and fewer horizontal rows of flounces, that her square shoulders should be downplayed with deep, round necklines that stopped short of the shoulders and would also emphasize her bosom.

Rosie hadn't ever considered that she had much of a bosom. But then, she had never worn dresses that revealed quite so much of it.

Fanny had chastised Rosie on her posture from the first day, and began at once to drill her on proper comportment and carriage. Throughout the fittings, she sent silent messages to Rosie reminding her to stand straight, to throw her shoulders back, to hold her head high. Rosie thought her neck too long and skinny and felt ridiculous stretching it out like a goose, but did as she was told.

She was shown fashion plates and sample garments, bolt after bolt of fabric, and trimming of every sort. She was draped and pinned and measured until she thought she might collapse from exhaustion. By the time they left the shop several hours later, Rosie had ordered morning dresses, promenade dresses, carriage dresses, evening dresses, and ball gowns, as well as capes, pelisses, and spencers. She had also procured an assortment of silk undergarments and several rather daring corsets that gave her more curves than she would have thought possible.

The next few days were spent buying slippers and stockings and gloves and reticules and bonnets and every other sort of accessory that Aunt Fanny thought necessary. And finally, the hairdresser was sent for. Monsieur Julien, her aunt told her, was the best and most famous coiffeur in London. Rosie felt as if she were meeting royalty and almost cowed under his Gallic glare. She let her hair down and stood rigid as he circled her, touching her hair and holding out a thick lock to examine it.

"Off!" he exclaimed. "All off. Eet eez too much."

Rosie experienced a moment of panic. What if he cut off all her hair and it looked horrible? Her desire to look fashionable would be thwarted, and there would be no time to grow it back. She chewed on her lower lip and considered the matter.

"You refuse to cut eet?" Monsieur Julien said, his voice raising in outrage. "Zen I leave. I cannot work weeth zeez . . . zeez mess."

"Please, Monsieur," Aunt Fanny said in her most charming tone, "do not be hasty. It is a big decision to cut off so much hair, is it not? You must be patient with Miss Lacey. She needs your skill with the scissors. I am certain she is willing to put herself in your hands, are you not, my dear?"

In for a penny, in for a pound. "Yes, of course," Rosie said. "Please do what you think best, Monsieur."

"Eet eez best to cut eet off," he said, and led her to a chair. "Eet eez too 'eavy and your face eez too narrow."

He draped a cloth about her shoulders, and within minutes the floor was thick with Rosie's hair. He continued to cut, using smaller scissors once the length had been chopped off. Rosie had worn her hair long all her life. The sudden absence of its weight, the cool air upon her neck, was positively liberating. She had no idea how it would look, but it felt wonderful.

Monsieur Julien stepped back and studied his work. "*Eh voilà!*" he said. "*Parfait.*"

Rosie glanced at her aunt who smiled and nodded her head. "It is wonderful," she said. "See for yourself."

Rosie took a deep breath before looking in the hand mirror she'd been given. When she did look, she almost failed to recognize the face in the reflection. Soft curls framed her cheeks and brow. Curls?

Monsieur's deft fingers primped and fluffed at his creation while Rosie continued to stare in disbelief. "Where did all these curls come from?" she asked. "You did not use an iron."

"Ze iron eez not *necessaire*. Ze curls are *naturelle*, Mademoiselle. Ze too long hair eez too 'eavy. Eet stretch ze curl straight. But Monsieur Julien make *parfait, non*?"

Rosie tilted her head from side to side as she admired her new look in the mirror. She could not keep the smile from her face. "Yes," she said. "It is indeed perfect. Thank you so much, Monsieur."

The Frenchman smiled and turned to Aunt Fanny. "She eez beautiful, *non?*"

"She is indeed."

And Rosie felt beautiful. Or close enough. Her nose was still too long and her mouth too wide and her cheeks too thin, but she felt almost beautiful for the first time in her life.

The next day, when she had dressed in one of her new evening frocks in preparation for Lady Wadsworth's rout, Rosie stared at her reflection in the pier glass and was pleased with what she saw. The dress was claret-colored crepe worn over a pink gossamer satin slip. The sleeves were short and full, composed of alternating panels of claret and pink, gathered into lattice-patterned bands of the same colors. A similar lattice band encircled the high waist. The bodice dipped shockingly low and revealed so much bosom that Rosie felt almost naked.

She could hardly believe the woman in the mirror was the same one who had left Devon only a week ago. That Rosie would never have dreamed of wearing such a dress in public and would likely have been frightened to death at the prospect of meeting friends of her notorious aunt. The new Rosie was looking forward to it. Perhaps she would meet more rakish gentlemen such as Mr. Davenant.

Tonight would be the true beginning of her adventure. She was attending her first Society event, wearing an elegant and sophisticated gown, and feeling ready to take on the world.

The new dress and hairstyle acted almost as a disguise. Or perhaps costume was a more accurate term, for donning it gave her the courage to act a part. At least for the short time she would be in London, she would not be the shy, plain, selfless older sister from Devon. She would play a new role: an elegant, sophisticated woman of the world. No longer Rosie, but Rosalind.

And Rosalind was ready for the curtain to rise on the first act.

She had never been to a rout and wasn't even quite sure what one was, but Fanny had assured her it was the best sort of gathering to begin her foray into Society. Rosie had been shown the invitation, which had simply said that Lord and Lady Wadsworth would be at home on Tuesday evening. It all sounded quite informal, and she worried that her dress was both too formal and too immodest for what sounded like a small gathering. Fanny had only laughed and told her she had a lot to learn about London Society.

She did indeed. She was astonished to discover that a rout was neither informal nor intimate.

It took them almost an hour to reach the Wadsworth townhouse, though it was only a handful of streets away from Fanny's residence on Berkley Square. There was an incredible crowd of carriages queuing up before the house. Every window of the palatial building was uncovered by either shutter or curtain to reveal a blaze of light within and what appeared to be a great assembly of people milling about.

Though it would have been easier to disembark and walk the few steps to the entrance, apparently that was simply not done. One waited one's turn and only left the carriage when it had reached the entrance.

Rosie's amazement continued once they had finally entered the house and mounted the grand staircase. It seemed that every room had been stripped bare of furniture, making room for a teeming crowd of beautifully dressed people. After being greeted by Lady Wadsworth, Rosie had stayed by Fanny's side as she made her slow way through the series of apartments. No one sat. There were no cards, no music, no dancing, and no food, though liveried waiters made their way through the crowds balancing trays of drinks. It was altogether a very odd affair, so far as Rosie was concerned. But oddly enjoyable.

Fanny introduced Rosie to more people than she could begin to remember, a great majority of them gentlemen. She could not help but notice an appreciative gleam in more than one gentleman's eye. It was surely the gown, with its scandalously low neckline and the modish shorter hem that revealed more than a hint of ankle. Or perhaps it was her new cropped hairstyle with the profusion of curls framing her face, confined by a demiturban hardly wider than a ribbon.

Whatever it was that brought so many approving glances, Miss Rosalind Lacey had become a center of attention. It was a heady experience for one who had never thought herself more than passably handsome.

She had done the right thing in coming to Aunt Fanny. Even if the disease took her tomorrow, it would have all been worth it.

Max moved through the crowd like an automaton. Every move, every look, every word had been performed a thousand times before. It was almost ritualistic in its sameness, but without the spiritual nourishment of ritual. In fact, it was all rather numbing to the spirit.

Sheer, unadulterated boredom.

One might ask why a man who so hated these wretched events continued to attend them. But Max had no need to ask himself such a question. Unfortunately, the answer was a predictable as the event itself.

Max always came looking for something new—something or someone to relieve the boredom, even for a moment. Something that might give him a reason not to take Freddie's route. But Max knew in his heart that what he sought did not exist. He'd seen it all, done it all, again and again. Nothing and no one piqued his interest anymore.

True, Max could easily find temporary escape in the arms of any number of willing women even now casting significant glances his way. No doubt he would. In fact, almost before realizing what he was doing, he answered Lady Heatherington's lifted brow with a discreet nod. She was a beautiful woman and a lively bed partner. And so, there would be momentary sport this evening after all.

But what of the morning?

He was tired of crawling out of some woman's bed before the sun rose, dressing in rumpled clothes, and making a hasty exit before dawn. He was tired of waking midday in his own bed, alone, with head throbbing from too much drink, the smell of stale perfume on his skin, and God knows how many vowels in his pockets.

Beautiful women practically at his beck and call. Sinfully lucky at the gaming tables. Money to burn and no obligations. Max was the envy of almost every man he knew.

Yet he felt old and tired and sick to death of his life.

It wasn't just the repetition. A good deal of what he did was worth repeating. An evening in Eugenia Heatherington's bed, for instance. No, it was something else that had begun to nag at him of late. Something that had never concerned him before, that only last year would have made him laugh if he had given it a single thought.

He was thirty-six years old and had done nothing with his life. There. He'd admitted it, if only to himself. His entire life he'd done nothing but womanize and drink and gamble, which had been enough until recently.

In fact, for quite some time debauchery had meant everything to him, had become his reason for existing. He had nothing else to live for, after all. Max had no career, no family, no charities, no interests. He supported himself by gambling, both in the hells and on the Exchange; and though he'd been rather successful, it wasn't much of a legacy.

Discounting the string of beauties he'd bedded over the years, the symbolic notches on his bedpost, there was nothing much Max had accomplished in his life, nothing he was proud of. Now, as he grew older, he had become bored by the pasha-like hedonism of his life.

There was only one reasonable thing to do when one's seemingly perfect life became intolerable. As he made his way through the crowd, he fingered Freddie's note and once again vowed that this would be his last Season.

Recollecting his assignation with Eugenia Heatherington, Max made a conscious effort to ignore all subsequent invitations, or at least to evade them. He did not have the energy for two intimate engagements tonight.

Lord, he *was* getting old. There had been a time—

"Max!"

His thoughts were cut short by the familiar voice somewhere to his left. He looked around but did not see her.

"Over here, Max."

Following the sound of her voice, he at last caught sight of a gold plume atop a spangled turban that could only have belonged to Fanny, and moved toward her. Perhaps she could help to brighten his dark mood.

Indeed, she could. He was prevented by the throng

of people from reaching her and was forced to stand
some distance away while he awaited a break in the
crowd. But he had a good view of her now, and could
see she was speaking to a young woman he'd never
seen. Someone new. Someone lovely. Someone who
smiled at him flirtatiously.

Bless Fanny's heart!

He inched his way along the stairway—he had not
yet even made it all the way inside to the main apartments—and kept his eye on the Unknown. She had
dark auburn hair that curled about her cheeks in a
most fetching manner. The ribbon threaded through
it was the same deep shade of red as her dress. She
had large eyes and full lips and the most beautiful
neck he'd ever seen. He wished the blasted crowd
would part so he could enjoy a full view of her, for
the one tantalizing glimpse he'd caught had revealed
a delicious swell of white bosom above the miniscule
bodice of the red dress.

She continued to smile at him, chuckling with
Fanny as though they shared some kind of joke. Her
smile was not shy or demure, but broad and uninhibited, more a grin than a smile. As he catalogued
her assets he could not help but note that the mouth
was considerably too wide and the nose a shade too
long for true beauty. There was, however, something
damnably provocative about that smile.

Had he not seen the smile, Max might have marked
her as a wide-eyed innocent. When she wasn't looking at him, her gaze seemed to devour the room, taking in every detail, every face, as though she were a
girl in her first Season whose Mama had never told
her it was gauche to gawk. But she was no young innocent. He was sure of it.

Who the devil was she?

Something about her seemed almost familiar, but
he was certain he'd never met her.

As he moved closer, he watched the Unknown cast her smile upon a gentleman who'd just approached from the opposite side. When he turned slightly, Max saw it was that coxcomb Alfie Hepworth. Damn the man, he was kissing her hand, and she was beaming at him.

Max gave a less then gentle shove to the young buck blocking his path, ignored the man's rude exclamation, and elbowed his way to Fanny's side.

"Max, darling, we thought you'd be stuck down there for hours. What a crush."

Max took her proffered hand and kissed the gloved fingers. "Good evening, Fanny. A vision, as always."

"Do you think so?" She lifted a hand to her headdress, setting gold spangles to jingle and dance. "I was not quite sure about this turban, you know. Thought it might look too much the mahjarani."

"It is charming, my dear. Have you just arrived?"

"Goodness, no. We were just leaving. Or trying to. We've been to Wadsworths' before coming here, and now we're off to Sir Reginald Forde's for a few hands of piquet."

As she spoke, Max could not keep his gaze from sliding over to the Unknown, who had not seemed to notice his arrival. Her entire attention, radiant smile and all, was focused on that fool Hepworth, damn his eyes.

"Max?"

When he returned his own attention to Fanny, she arched a questioning brow. "Would you like to come along with us to Forde's? Eldridge will be there to see us home, of course, so you needn't worry about that. But we would welcome your escort, if you'd be so obliging."

"I am ever at your service, Fanny. And of your lovely young friend." He lowered his voice and spoke directly into her ear. "Introduce us, my dear, I beg you."

Fanny began to laugh. "Ha! We *knew* you hadn't recognized her." Her blue eyes danced with merriment.

"Recognized her? Do I know her?" He kept his voice low in hopes the woman would not overhear. "No. No, Fanny, I am quite sure I've never met her."

"Are you?" She reached over and touched the Unknown's arm. "Excuse me, my dear, but you remember Max Davenant, do you not?"

The woman looked at him and smiled. "Yes, of course. How do you do, Mr. Davenant? So nice to see you again."

She offered her hand and he took it, still thoroughly confounded. Who *was* she? "Your servant, madam."

He studied her more closely without letting go of her hand, and could not help but notice that she seemed perfectly willing to allow him to keep hold of it. He had been right. She was no demure young miss. The mere fact that she was with Fanny told him that much. Despite that intriguing aura of innocence about her, there was a decidedly flirtatious twinkle in her eyes.

Something about those eyes . . .

"I say, Davenant," Hepworth said as he inched closer to the Unknown, "I ought to have known you'd steal a march on the rest of us with Miss Lacey. Fanny's niece and all. Unfair advantage, what?"

Miss Lacey? Fanny's niece?

The mouse?

Chapter 4

She ought to have been exhausted. It was past two in the morning, but Rosie didn't feel the least bit tired. The evening had been so full of excitement for her that she still felt agog with it all. When they finally went home, she doubted she would be able to sleep a wink.

Her head was spinning with introductions and flattery and flirtations. When she had first begun planning her trip to London, she had hoped there might be a remote possibility of attracting at least one gentleman's regard. Not with the usual goal of marriage, of course, but only to experience it, to know what it was like to have a gentleman admire her. More than admire, actually. She longed for more than that. After all, she had added "to be thoroughly kissed" to her list of things to do in London.

Giddy with a first night's success, Rosie thought it might not be the impossible goal she had once imagined.

Upon reflection, she was genuinely amazed at what she had been able to accomplish as Rosalind. The old Rosie would have quivered in her slippers to have endured the often presumptuous addresses of so many gentlemen—from fresh-faced young fops to seasoned rakes to aging roués. The old Rosie would likely have swooned at the way Lord Radcliffe used the crowd to allow himself to brush up against her, at the way Mr. Hepworth had teased open the buttons of her glove in order to stroke the skin of her wrist, at the way Mr. Davenant had boldly held her hand in his for longer than was absolutely proper. Such gentlemen, and such behavior, would have frightened the old Rosie almost to death.

But not Rosalind. *She* had rather enjoyed it.

Too distracted to concentrate on cards, Rosie had excused herself from the last hand, retrieved her shawl, and wandered onto the terrace. She leaned against the balustrade overlooking a moonlit garden below, and retrieved the notebook from her reticule. She began to check off a few entries from her list, those objectives she had so far succeeded in accomplishing: to wear a beautiful dress, to have her hair cut and fashionably styled, to be admired by a gentleman—she was reasonably sure most of the men she'd met were gentlemen. Even Fanny's friends must be gentlemen.

And she grinned as she checked off her latest item, "to flirt with a rake." Yes, she had flirted, and not only with Mr. Davenant but with other men who must surely be rakes. Rosie supposed she still had a lot to learn about flirtation, but she had made a start and had thoroughly enjoyed herself. It was quite liberating to realize she could, for the most part, behave exactly as she pleased without worrying about the consequences.

At the sound of footsteps approaching, she turned to see Mr. Davenant walking toward her. She returned the notebook to its case and dropped it in her reticule, then smiled up at him as he leaned back against the balustrade beside her.

"You're still laughing at me, Miss Lacey. Were you making a note in your diary about my foolish behavior this evening?"

Her smile widened, but she refrained from laughing. She and Fanny had already teased the poor man relentlessly earlier in the evening. "I am merely smiling, Mr. Davenant, as you see."

"Maybe so," he said, and offered a smile of his own that made him look even more devilishly handsome. "But you don't fool me. You are laughing inside. I cannot tell you how thrilled I am to have been such a source of amusement for you and Fanny."

She lost the battle with restraint and began to laugh softly. "You can hardly blame us, sir. The look upon your face was priceless."

"No doubt. But you can hardly blame me, either, my dear, when you look so completely different from the way you did at that first brief meeting. By God, you seemed the perfect little brown mouse."

"I know."

"And now." He paused and gave her a look that sent a shiver dancing up and down her spine. "Now, you look quite lovely. Not even remotely mouselike. Red becomes you, my dear."

His voice wrapped around her like thick velvet. No wonder the man was notorious. He was a spellbinder, drawing one in with his sumptuous voice and his liquid brown eyes. What would it be like to succumb to his spell? Should she try? She stifled a giggle at the very notion of plain Rosie Lacey as an object of seduction, much less succumbing to it. Ursula would faint dead away on the spot.

Heavens, but she was having a good time as Rosalind! If things had turned out differently, she might have had a successful career on the stage.

"Thank you, Mr. Davenant," she said in a husky whisper she sincerely hoped sounded provocative and not sickly. "That is a very pretty compliment."

"Call me Max," he said in that velvety voice. "I'm practically family, you know."

"Then you must call me Rosi—Rosalind."

"'Let no fair be kept in mind, but the fair of Rosalind.' I trust this fair Rosalind need not resort to disguise to win her heart's desire." Rosie almost gasped at his words. Did he know she merely played a part? "Fanny must be pleased," he went on, oblivious to her momentary uneasiness. "You were quite the hit this evening."

Rosie pulled herself together and allowed Rosalind to take charge once again. "Yes, I am sure my aunt was pleased that people were so friendly to her niece."

"That is not what I meant."

"Oh?"

"By George, but you do know how to play the innocent, don't you? It is no wonder you have every buck and beau dangling after you. And that is the point, is it not? To bring one of them up to scratch?"

"I beg your pardon?"

"The Marriage Mart, my dear. You are older than the other young chits, to be sure, but you do have a way about you. Since we are almost family, I am sure you will not mind such frank speaking. In any case, I cannot imagine you will have any difficulty finding a husband."

Rosie's first reaction was to be insulted by his words, her next to be flattered by them, but in the end she found the entire situation hilarious and began to laugh.

"You do not believe me?" Max asked.

When she was finally able to speak, she said, "I'm afraid you have it all wrong, Mr. Davenant. Max. In the first place, I do not know how a liaison between my aunt and your father makes us family." His brows rose in surprise at her words. Did he think she did not know? "Unless, of course, you are really my aunt's son and therefore my cousin, though I feel certain Aunt Fanny would have mentioned it. That is, unless it is a great dark secret that she has kept all these years. No, no, that cannot be, for I find it impossible to imagine she would have allowed your Mama to raise her son."

Now Max was on the verge of laughter, a grin creasing his face and lighting his eyes. "In the second place," she continued, "I am *not* in search of a husband. I realize that notion will occur to most people, but I wish it would not. In fact, I have no intention of ever marrying. That is not why I came to London."

"Why did you come, then?"

"To have fun. To enjoy myself. To go to balls and dance all night until my slippers wear out, to go to elegant supper parties and dine on rich food and fine wine, to attend the theater and the opera and philharmonic concerts, to visit museums and galleries and gardens and parks and shops—dear heaven, the shops!—and the Tower and Westminster Abbey and Astley's and Vauxhall and, oh, all sorts of other places I've yet to discover." Her voice rose with excitement, just thinking about all the things she was going to do. "I want to see everything, do everything, to experience *everything* London has to offer."

"Odds fish, madam," he said, and placed a limp hand upon his forehead. "I grow dizzy just listening to you. Let us sit down before I collapse with fatigue."

He led her to a stone bench beside a potted box shrub trimmed to a perfect sphere. When Rosie had seated herself and arranged her skirts, Max sat down beside her. Not too close, she noticed. In fact, he sat as far away as possible without actually teetering on the far edge.

"And so you are keen to enjoy town pleasures?"

"I am all agog."

He chuckled. "Indeed you are. Your eyes fairly dance in anticipation. I suspect you must be younger than you look."

"I am six and twenty."

"As elderly as that? Astonishing. At so ancient an age, how have you managed to maintain so much . . . lust for life?" He lingered over the word *lust*, caressing the sound of each letter so that Rosie could not take her eyes away from his mouth. He was trying to rattle her. She did not believe he truly meant to seduce her, only to test her, to see what would make her squirm. She would not give him the pleasure of victory.

"It is my first visit to London," she said with perfect equanimity. "Everything is new to me."

"Ah, yes. Of course. To be in one's first Season when all is fresh and untried. How I envy you, my dear. Enjoy the novelty while you can."

"While I can. Yes."

He gave a weary sigh. "Alas, I have too many Seasons behind me. I have been everywhere and done everything—countless times, over and over. It begins to pall." His hand moved upon his breast as if protecting something tucked away in his waistcoat.

"I do not believe you," Rosie said. His head jerked up at her words. She was rather surprised at them herself; but Rosalind was in charge now and Rosalind could say anything she pleased. "My aunt has told me of your reputation, sir."

"Warned you against me, did she?"

"No. She simply mentioned it as a point of fact. But if it's true, then it seems as though you cannot be as bored as you pretend. I would guess you manage to find a good deal of pleasure in Society. Quite a lot of it, actually. I sincerely doubt that such . . . such gratification has begun to pall."

"You'd be surprised," he muttered.

"I'll wager you have interesting plans of your own for the Season," she said. "Tell me about them."

"Egad, you want names?"

Rosie flushed. "I did not mean *those* sorts of plans.

I am just curious about all the types of entertainments London has to offer. It seems there is *so* much to do. There must be something you are looking forward to."

"Not really," he said. There was a hint of resignation in his tone that made her believe him, and she was surprised at how angry it made her. Here was the consummate pleasure-seeker, with years and years of pleasure stretching ahead of him, while she only had these few months in which to find her own enjoyment. How dare he take his life for granted!

"You are not happy, Mr. Davenant?" she asked.

"I have never sought happiness, my dear, only pleasure."

"And found it?"

"Often. Too often."

"Have you never been in love, then?"

"Only for brief moments, in the heat of passion. Fortunately, it always passes."

His callous words increased her annoyance with him. He had so much to live for, and yet did not grab hold of a single moment as meaningful or lasting. He did not look beyond momentary pleasure to find something deeper, something special. A wasted life.

He must have sensed her irritation, for he straightened slightly and offered a sheepish smile. "All right," he said, "you asked if I had plans. Well, I do. If you must know, there is a mill next week that has piqued my interest."

"A mill?"

"Yes, Randall and Neate. Should be great sport. But I don't imagine that is the sort of entertainment you had in mind."

"But I've never been to a mill. All of my brothers are mad for them. To tell you the truth, I should love to see one. Just once."

"Ah, but Fair Rosalind, think how Society would frown upon such unladylike behavior."

"Oh, pooh! As if I care a fig for what Society thinks of me. I simply want to experience everything I can while I'm here. In town, I mean."

"Brave words, my dear. But do you not worry about your reputation?"

She might have at one time. But what did it matter now? "No," she replied, and rose from the bench. "I am not concerned for my reputation."

Max stood and said, "You ought not say something so enticing to a man like me." He leaned close, so close she could feel his breath upon her neck. "You might experience a great deal more than you expected."

Rosie offered her broadest smile, then walked toward the terrace doors. When she reached them, she looked over her shoulder in the most coquettish manner she could muster, and said, "Why, Mr. Davenant, you have no idea what I expect."

She entered the drawing room without waiting to see if her attempt at flirtation had succeeded.

Max studied the sway of her hips beneath the red skirts as she walked away from him. The minx! Not only had he been thoroughly captivated by Rosalind's artless charm, but he was quite sure that within the week half the male population of London would be smitten as well.

Despite her rejection of the notion, Max did rather think of her as family, and determined to watch out for her. She may appear to others to be an experienced flirt, up to every rig and row. But Max knew from Fanny that the girl had been stuck in the country her whole life and therefore could not possibly be as sophisticated as she let on. She was sure to get herself in trouble if she wasn't careful.

Knowing she was an untried rustic, Max had no intention of being the instrument of that trouble. He did not for one moment believe her denial about coming to town in search of a husband. She spoke of love, after all. What woman spoke of love without thoughts of marriage? Rosalind, despite her words to the contrary, was no different from the rest. All unmarried women, with the possible exception of the professional Cyprians, were in search of a husband. If he even so much as kissed the girl, he would be in the untenable position of having seduced the daughter of Fanny's stiff-rumped brother. The man would put a bullet in Max's head if he refused to "do the right thing."

And no pistol-in-the-ribs forced wedding, either, thank you very much. He shuddered just to think of it. No, such a fate was not for Max, so he would steer clear of Miss Lacey and her considerable attractions.

Yet, she was Fanny's niece, and poor Fanny would be the one forced to deal with whatever mischief Rosalind fell into. Max adored Fanny and had no wish to see her saddled with such an irksome chore. So, he would keep an eye on the girl. For Fanny's sake.

It was a difficult assignment. Over the next week, Rosalind flitted about town with that come-hither smile and those hazel eyes wide in innocent wonder. Such a paradox could not help but intrigue any man who spent more than five minutes in her company. And Max was quite sure that Rosalind remained perfectly unconscious of her power.

"Are you absolutely certain she is Sir Edmund's daughter," he asked Fanny a few nights after the Forde card party, "and not some imposter come to town to take advantage of you?" They stood together along the edge of the ballroom at Almack's, a place Max generally avoided and Fanny detested. But Rosalind had begged to go and Fanny had capitulated. In a moment of weakness, Max had agreed to accompany them.

They watched as Rosalind gathered a circle of gallants around her. She laughed and flirted and teased and wielded her fan with remarkable finesse. Where had she learned to do that?

Fanny chuckled. "No one is more astonished than I am to find such spirit in the girl."

Rosalind gave an uninhibited crack of laughter that caused many heads to turn, and she swatted young Lord Radcliffe on the arm with her fan. Several older women directed stern looks in Rosalind's direction, but Max noted that most of the gentlemen in the vicinity smiled.

Fanny smiled, too, looking for all the world like a proud mother hen as Rosalind was led into a quadrille by Sir Cedric Bassett. "Max, darling, is she not delightful? You know how I dreaded her arrival. I don't know how I could have been so wrong about her, but I tell you she is not at all as I remembered her. Quiet. Reserved. Plain, even. Lord, she's not plain at all, is she, Max?"

"Dash it, Fanny, you're as bad as any marriage-minded mama trotting out her chick, shamelessly angling for compliments. It must be this horrid place. The deuced lemonade has gone to your head."

"I shall feel obliged to slap you, Max, if you persist in comparing me to those ravenous matrons. I am no more pleased to be in this odious place than you are, but she would insist. I merely wondered how you thought she looked."

"She looks lovely."

"She does, doesn't she?" Fanny crooned. "It's remarkable considering . . . Well, you saw her when she arrived."

"You've done a marvelous job with her, my dear."

"Oh, it was not my doing. Not entirely, anyway. I

did select that emerald figured silk, though, as well as the cunning little aigrette in her hair. The color suits her, don't you think? It brings out the—"

"Green flecks in her eyes. I noticed."

She arched a brow. "I ought to have known you would notice, Max. Must I prepare a lecture for my niece on the dangers of the infamous Max Davenant?"

"That will not be necessary. I would never do that to you, my dear. I was simply admiring all you have done for her. I do indeed remember her arrival. I thought her the drabbest mouse."

"Do you know on that very first day she announced to me that she wished to be transformed? She knew she looked the mouse and wanted so desperately to be stylish. But even the most fashionable dresses could not have disguised a vapid disposition. From the first, though, she has shown such gumption, such spark, such—"

"Such a wild desire to experience everything."

"Yes! You've noticed it, too? I declare, a sort of mad curiosity, an exquisite wonder, fairly throbs in her veins. Oh Max, she reminds me so much of myself at a younger age—much younger even than Rosalind. Poor thing, how Edmund must have stifled her spirit all these years. I could strangle the man. No wonder she wanted to come to town. She must have been bursting to escape before it was too late."

"Too late?"

"She is six and twenty, Max."

"Too late for a Season? Too late to find a husband? But she tells me she is not looking for a husband."

Fanny gave a dismissive wave of her hand. "Yes, I know. She has told me the same thing, over and over again. The odd thing is, I believe she means it."

"I got the same impression."

When the quadrille ended, Max saw Rosalind make her way toward them and he rose to allow her his place on the bench. She sank down upon it in a swirl of green silk, breathless, and worked her fan with enough vigor to stir up a respectable gust.

"Heavens, but it has become warm in here. I really do not know why my sisters thought this place so wonderful."

"You appeared to be enjoying yourself," Max said.

"Well, there are always interesting people everywhere one goes in London, are there not? But all things considered—the décor, the food, the music—this place is really nothing very special. In fact, it's a trifle dull. Especially compared to some of the other parties we've attended."

Fanny rose to her feet and shook out her skirts. "Rosalind, my dear, you are a woman after my own heart. If you are quite satisfied that you have seen enough of Almack's, let us be off to the Sanbourne ball. It is sure to be more entertaining."

As they gathered at the King Street entrance to meet Max's carriage, the strains of a waltz could be heard from within the assembly hall. "Oh, blast!" Rosalind exclaimed. "Wouldn't you know they'd play a waltz now, just when we're leaving. I was so hoping to dance one."

"It is just as well," Fanny said as she was handed into the carriage. "You have yet not received permission to waltz."

Rosalind looked sharply at her aunt. "Permission? I must have permission to waltz? From whom, may I ask? From you, aunt?"

"Heavens, no! Why should it matter to me? No, it is those blasted patronesses who rule Almack's."

"They can decide who dances what?" Rosalind's eyes grew wide with indignation.

"They decide everything in regard to Almack's, including who can attend," Max said. "Did you not know what strings your poor aunt had to pull in order to get tonight's tickets? All attendees must have the blessing of one of the patronesses."

"Fanny! Is that true? I knew is was rather exclusive, but I had not realized it was so restricted. And tell me why you, of all people, should have trouble getting vouchers? You are Lady Parkhurst, after all."

"I have not always been welcome within the fine portals of Almack's," Fanny said. "Earlier patronesses barred me from the door. Very high sticklers, don't you know. These new ones are even worse, if you ask me. But my more notorious days are behind me and these new patronesses are young women who were not even born when I was kicking up my heels. With a bit of cajolery and sweet talk, I was able to wheedle the vouchers out of Emily Cowper." Fanny gave a self-satisfied chuckle. "I could see, though, that Sally Jersey was not pleased to see me. That woman wouldn't allow her own mother-in-law in the door."

"Outrageous!" Rosalind said. Her eyes blazed with anger and Max thought her especially lovely under that new fire. "You should not have to beg for patronage. You are better than the lot of them put together, I should imagine. How dare they!"

Max noted Fanny's flush of pride at Rosalind's words. He thanked heaven, not for the first time, that the tiresome wretch of a niece Fanny had expected had instead turned out to be this vibrant woman so full of spirit.

"They dare," Fanny was saying, "because they are puffed up with their own consequence."

"They sound just like my Uncle Talmadge. Horrid man."

"Lord Talmadge is your uncle?" Max asked. "He of the anti-reform speeches and morality pamphlets?"

"The very one."

"Egad, Fanny, you never told me you were related to Talmadge."

"I'm not, thank God."

"He is my mother's brother," Rosalind said. "He has always been hateful to my family because . . . well, just because. Anyway, these Almack's women sound just as hateful! Making you beg their indulgence. Hmph!"

"Do not waste a single thought on those harridans, my girl," Fanny said. "It doesn't bother me in the least. I have never cared about their wretched little assemblies with their weak lemonade and mediocre music and dull company. They are none of them even worthy of my contempt."

"Jealous prigs," Max said.

"I believe you must be right," Rosalind said, looking across at Max. "They must lead horribly dull lives and feel obliged to tell others how to behave in order to lend themselves some kind of importance. Jealous prigs, indeed! Mr. Davenant, I declare were we not already several streets away, I would have you turn this coach around, return us to King Street where I would drag you onto the dance floor and force you to waltz with me. I have never danced the waltz, but I feel sure you could teach me."

"Indeed, I could."

"Fanny, we must contrive to get tickets again next Wednesday. And you must come along, Mr. Davenant, and lead me out for a waltz. Will you promise?"

"Fanny will have my head if I help you to ruin your reputation, my dear."

"I will do no such thing," Fanny said. "What harm is a simple waltz, anyway?"

"And I am not sixteen," Rosalind added as the carriage came to a halt in front of Sanbourne house. "At my age, I am far less likely to cause a single head to turn if I dare to waltz. Except, hopefully, for those horrid patronesses whose rules I am simply itching to defy. Odious women! Will you promise me, Mr. Davenant?"

"All right, minx." His footman opened the carriage door and Max stepped out, then turned to hand down the ladies. "But you must promise me," he said to Rosalind, "that you will call me Max."

"Oh yes, you must cease this Mr. Davenant business, my dear," Fanny said, shaking out her skirts and adjusting her plumes. "Max is practically family, you know."

Rosalind caught his eye and grinned, obviously recollecting their previous conversation, and he gave her a wink.

When he offered an arm to lead her up the stairs, she winked back.

Chapter 5

Rosie stood on the pavement before Fanny's town-house and only half listened to the inane chatter of Mr. Jeremy Aldrich who stood beside her. They had been introduced and had danced together at the Sanbourne ball, and he had been overly attentive ever since. Frankly, Rosie found his youthful prattle tiresome and would not have given him the time of day were it not for his invitation to ride in the park.

In his brand-new sporting vehicle.

If nothing else, young Mr. Aldrich would allow her to check off one more item from her list. Actually, the item had been amended to say "drive" and not simply "ride" in a sporting vehicle, but Rosie would not broach that subject just yet.

The list should have been getting smaller as more and more items had been checked off. She had been to Almack's, had danced all night at a grand private ball, had drunk champagne, had received flowers from admirers. That last had not actually been on the list, but it ought to have been. It was most gratifying to find the drawing room filled with bouquets the morning after the Sanbourne ball.

But the list actually grew longer as she added more items to it each day. To attend a masque wearing some sort of daring costume. To take snuff. To look up her uncle Talmadge and tell him exactly what she thought of him. And to defy the Almack's ladies and dance

the waltz. With Max, of course. If she was going to
tweak the noses of the lady patronesses, she might as
well do it with a handsome and notorious rake.

She had spent the last dozen years doing all that
was proper, acting the very paragon of responsibility.
During these few short months left her, it was exhil-
arating to do and say exactly what she pleased, to
throw propriety and respectability to the winds. Lord,
but she was having fun!

She wondered what Mr. Aldrich would say if he
knew she intended to take the reins of his bang-up
new curricle and see if she could make it fly?

The young tiger maneuvered the vehicle to a halt
in front of them, then jumped down to hold the horses
in place. They danced about skittishly, anxious to be
off. Rosie knew exactly how they felt.

"It *is* a beauty, isn't it?" Mr. Aldrich said. "The *sang
de boeuf* color is sure to be all the crack. I designed
the polished brass fittings myself. See how the design
incorporates my cypher? Clever, eh? You will note
that even the bar is polished brass. It is perfectly bal-
anced and sprung. And the upholstery is the finest
Morocco leather. I assure you, Miss Lacey, no expense
was spared in the construction."

All the while he yammered on, his young tiger held
the horses—a beautiful matched pair of chestnut
bays—and Rosie could think of nothing but how much
she wished he would be quiet and hand her up into
the thing so they could be off.

"And the improved method of suspension—"

"Yes, Mr. Aldrich," Rosie interrupted, "it is surely
a fine piece of machinery and I am all agog to see
how it performs. Now, hand me up please before I
am overcome with excitement."

He gave her an indulgent smile. "Your excitement
is quite understandable. Allow me? Up you go, then."

When Mr. Aldrich sat down beside her, and then

the tiger leapt up onto his seat behind, Rosie giggled at the bouncing motion. The jaunty little carriage was so buoyant, it was like sitting in a feather bed. She could not suppress the desire to bounce up and down—just a little. It really was incredibly springy.

"Are you quite all right, Miss Lacey?"

"Indeed I am, Mr. Aldrich. Just testing the springs. This is a perfectly marvelous curricle. I adore it."

"I knew you would," he said, a smug grin upon his face. "Let us be off, then."

After a few moments of an exquisitely smooth but otherwise uneventful ride, Rosie boldly rested her hand on Mr. Aldrich's arm. He smiled triumphantly and placed a hand over hers. Her fingers, though, crept down to his hand that held the reins.

"You *are* going to give me a chance at the ribbons, are you not, Mr. Aldrich? Jeremy?"

His back stiffened and his hand tightened over hers. "You . . . you want to drive?"

"How could I not? It is such a splendid vehicle. You will make me the envy of every woman—to be seen driving a slap up to the mark carriage, with such a handsome man at my side. Please, Mr. Aldrich? Jeremy?"

He squirmed beside her. "I . . . I don't know, Miss Lacey."

"You must call me Rosalind," she purred.

"Rosalind." He spoke her name like a prayer and gazed at her with such calf's eyes it was all she could do not to giggle. "Rosalind. But . . . but, do you know how to drive a team?"

"I have been driving for years." She would not mention that she had only ever driven an old dog cart with a single sluggish nag. But how hard could it be to manage two horses?

"You think you could handle this team?" Jeremy asked.

She gave him her most adoring look and crooned into his ear. "I'm sure you could teach me what I need to know, Jeremy."

The young man was ridiculously susceptible to flirtation. Or perhaps she had simply gotten better at it. She had watched her aunt closely and taken note of her technique. Though she was older even than Rosie's father, Aunt Fanny could wrap any man of any age around her finger. It had been easy enough to learn how to flirt. You simply made each man believe he was the center of your world. It almost didn't matter what words you said, so long as you gazed deeply into his eyes and gave him your whole attention.

Jeremy Aldrich had succumbed in an instant.

When he had negotiated the streets of Mayfair and reached the park entrance, he handed the reins to Rosie. She allowed him to take her hands in his and guide her in handling the ribbons.

After a few minutes, she asked, "May I try on my own now, Jeremy?"

"You're sure?"

"Quite sure."

"All right, then. Be careful, Rosalind. The horses are fresh."

And then she was driving on her own, bouncing along on the Morocco leather seat, the horses following her lead, Jeremy beaming at her. It was wonderful. It was exciting.

It was too slow.

She flicked the reins and urged the horses on.

"I say, Rosalind, you might not want to go quite so fast. The park can be crowded this time of day."

"Then let's go this way." She steered the team away from the main paths and into the open space, then urged them on faster. And faster. And faster.

"Rosalind! What are you doing?"

"I'm flying!" And she was. With the wind in her

face and the well-sprung carriage beneath her, she felt as though she could take off straight up into the sky. She gave a whoop of pure joy.

Jeremy laughed nervously beside her. "Perhaps you had better let me take the ribbons now, Rosalind."

"I'm having too much fun!" She shrugged off his hands when he tried to grab the reins from her.

"If you won't give me the ribbons, then I must insist that you pull up." There was a hint of anxiety beneath his stern tone. "*Now*, Rosalind. Before we have an accident."

She had no intention of having an accident, but it was his brand-new curricle, after all. She could understand his apprehension. Especially when she began to notice people scattering all in directions.

Though she had deliberately avoided the throngs of strollers and riders along the main paths, they behaved as though they believed the team was out of control and would mow them down. Blast. She was in perfect control. Her father and brother had taught her well. It was easy. If she had been at home she could have flown like the wind for miles down deserted country roads. But if she was at home, she would never have had the opportunity to drive such a fine, sleek vehicle. Blast and double blast.

With a sigh of resignation, Rosie pulled back the reins and expertly guided the team to the edge of the Serpentine. The horses, however, did not stop as she had expected but seemed headed straight for the water.

"Rosalind!"

She gave the reins a wild jerk in the opposite direction, and the team came to a sudden, jolting halt, tossing the little tiger out of his seat in back.

Assured the boy was unharmed when he scampered up from the grass, Rosie threw back her head and laughed. It was jubilant, exultant laughter, for the sheer reckless thrill of the ride. Good Lord, but that had been fun. She looked over to find Jeremy staring at her open-mouthed. "Are you mad?" he asked.

"I don't believe so," she replied, and continued to chuckle softly.

"No," Jeremy said, and then took her hands in his. Rosie was astonished to find him gazing ardently into her eyes. She had thought him angry. "No, you are not mad," he said. "But I am mad for you, my dear Rosalind. I declare, you are more exciting than any woman I've ever known. Pluck to the backbone. All the rest are nothing more than simpering, faint-hearted little chits in comparison. But you, my dear Rosalind, you are magnificent."

Rosie thought he might have kissed her then and there—and she would have let him—had not a small crowd begun to gather around the curricle. Curse it! To be thoroughly kissed after such a thrilling ride— now *that* would have been a day to remember.

"Outstanding, Miss Lacey!" Sir Cedric Bassett said as he approached. "Never seen a female drive so well in all my life."

Max slowed his approach when he saw the others surround the vehicle, and could see clearly that Rosalind was unhurt. In fact, she was laughing.

"Don't look like she needs rescuing to me." Sir George Fellowes had been strolling with Max along the Chesterfield Gate footpath, taking stock of the afternoon's population of attractive females, when the shiny red curricle had sped past. Max had recognized Rosalind at once, seen that she held the reins, and assumed she had lost control of the team. Tugging his friend along, he hurried after the carriage with some vague notion of helping to avert danger.

He ought to have known better.

"Well, thank God for that," Max said and waved

a hand in front of his face like a fan. "Heroics are much too exhausting."

Fellowes laughed. "Don't believe I ever saw you move so fast, Davenant."

"A momentary madness, I assure you."

"You ain't hanging out for The Lacey, are you?"

"Hanging out?" Max made a great show of looking over his clothing to make sure all was in place. "Egad, I hope not. What a vulgar notion, Fellowes."

"Wouldn't want to move in if you'd already staked a claim, that's all."

"I beg your pardon?"

"Well . . . several of us thought you might be involved, you know. Seen with her a lot, and all that."

Good Lord. This was not a rumor he wanted to see bandied about town. The girl's reputation would be in tatters. "My dear old chap," he said in his most bored tone, "the chit is Fanny's niece, fresh from the country. The rustic types don't appeal to me in the least."

"Nothing rustic about The Lacey." Max turned at the familiar voice of Lord Nicholas Vaughn, who fell into step beside him. "Seems to know a thing or two, that one."

"Just what I thought," Fellowes said. "Lively as they come. I don't care if she *is* from the country, I'd lay odds the woman knows what's what, unmarried or not. She has this way of looking at a man—"

"Don't she, though?" Vaughn said. "I'd give a monkey to find out what's behind that smile."

"You and everyone else in town," Fellowes said. "Except old Davenant here, apparently."

"On behalf of every man in London," Vaughn said, "I thank you, Davenant, for pulling out of the race. Without your irresistible charm and diabolical good looks, the rest of us may, for once, stand a chance."

"Have a care, gentlemen," Max said, feeling thoroughly uneasy at the direction the conversation was taking. "I do not believe Miss Lacey is quite as up to snuff as you may think. Fanny assures me she has led a quiet life in the country until now."

"And the nut never falls too far from the tree, does it?" Vaughn said. "With Lady Parkhurst as her aunt, and apparently her 'chaperone' as well, it is only to be expected if the girl's a high flyer."

Max flinched at his friend's words. "I really don't think—"

"Overheard her tell Lady Samantha Kirby that she ain't looking for a husband, only wants to have fun," Fellowes said.

"I've heard much the same," said Vaughn. "And that seems to be precisely what she's doing. A chip off the aunt's block, if you ask me."

"I don't believe I did ask, actually," Max muttered.

"Pretty woman, too," Vaughn continued. "A bit tall, but very nicely put together. Never saw such a delectable neck. Love to work my way down it, what?"

"Egad!" Max exclaimed.

"I say, Vaughn," Fellowes said, "I believe I spoke first. Since Davenant ain't interested—"

"Then it's every man for himself," Vaughn said. "She don't seem to favor any one in particular anyway. Look at that mob. Every single one of 'em thinks she is flirting with him alone. But she don't play favorites. Dangles 'em all with equal promise. Now, I ask you, Davenant, what's a man to think?"

What, indeed? thought Max. Either he had the girl pegged all wrong, or she was headed for serious trouble. If she was in fact an innocent and every rake and rogue in town thought her otherwise, she might find herself in the soup before long. Fanny would have to pack her off back to Devon and her starchy father; and if what Max had heard of the man were true, he would like as not throw her out on her ear.

On the other hand, what if Max had simply been blinded by the perpetual wonder in those big hazel eyes, when it was the sensual mouth that marked her true character? Did every other man see what he didn't? Could she in fact be more like Fanny than he'd thought?

Max wondered if Fanny had been altogether honest with him regarding Rosalind. She seemed to delight in throwing them together, and she knew full well that he'd never had a respectable intention in all his life. Was Fanny simply setting him up for quick fling? Was she perhaps seeing Max and Rosalind as a reflection of herself and his father, joining them as sort of book-ended liaisons spanning the decades in perfect symmetry?

Well, by Jove, if that's what was afoot Max would be happy to oblige. Though certainly not the most beautiful woman he'd ever known, Rosalind was definitely one of the most intriguing. If he thought for one minute she was after nothing more than a quick liaison in town, he wanted to be the one to accommodate her. She shouldn't have to settle for Vaughn or Fellowes or any one of those barbarians surrounding Aldrich's curricle. She should have the best. She should have Max.

As they neared the curricle, Max could not help but notice the scornful looks of respectable matrons leading their young charges away from Rosalind's laughter as she sat surrounded by a thong of adoring bucks and beaux. Were they outraged by her uninhibited enjoyment, or by the fact that she drew the attention of so many young men away from their daughters? In either case, Rosalind was winning no friends among Society's high sticklers.

When the three men reached the edge of the crowd, Rosalind looked up and saw Max. She smiled broadly and waved to him.

"Max!" she called out and the crowd of men reluctantly parted to allow him access. "Did you see? Did you see me fly?"

"Indeed I did, minx. I thought for a moment you might take a nose dive straight into the Serpentine. My nerves will never be the same, I assure you. I shall require at least a week's rest to recover."

"Jeremy," she said, leaning over to her proud young swain, "would you mind terribly if I stepped down for just the tiniest moment and walked a short way with Max? I have something particular to say to him."

Aldrich did not look pleased, but obviously had no desire to appear the possessive cad and nodded his acquiescence.

"I promise to be back in two shakes," she said, smiling sweetly at the young man. "Hand me down, Max, if you please."

To the frustrated groans and protests from her admirers, all of whom were jockeying for position to do the honors, Rosalind placed her hands on Max's shoulders and allowed him to lift her down from the curricle. Young Aldrich shot Max a look of such venom that he felt sure he ought to expect a formal challenge from the young man.

"Your young swain is not happy, my dear," he whispered in her ear as he led her slightly away from the crowd. He was not surprised to find Fellowes and Vaughn among the disappointed assembly. He was, though, surprised to discover how thoroughly cocky he felt that Rosalind had singled him out from the teeming hoards. It had been years since he hadn't taken such distinction for granted. "I believe he hoped to have you all to himself," he said.

"Absurd!" she replied, and laughed.

"Yes, I daresay it is absurd. How can he have you to himself with a dozen other gentlemen vying for your attention?"

"Do you know that Mr. Newcombe has offered to let me drive his cabriolet? And Lord Radcliffe wants me to test his new curricle? Isn't that marvelous?"

"My dear minx, you will continue to scandalize all those proper matrons who are shooting disparaging looks your way as we speak."

She quickly glanced in the direction of a glowering Lady Sommerville, then gave a dismissive wave of her hand—a gesture so like her aunt that Max once again began to wonder about the true nature of this young woman.

"Actually, the scandalized matrons brings me to what I wanted to speak to you about," she said.

"Indeed?"

"I hope you have not forgotten your promise. Wednesday is fast approaching and I plan to attend Almack's. I shall expect that waltz."

"You are determined to thumb your nose at the lady patronesses, are you not?"

"Well, it still aggravates me that they dare question my aunt's request for vouchers. I would certainly not mind thumbing my nose at them. But that is not why I want you to remember your promise."

"Oh?"

"I simply want to waltz," she said, amusement twinkling in her eyes. "With you, Max. You did promise."

"My dear minx, there is a legion of men right here in the park who would be willing to lead you out onto the floor, patronesses be damned."

"Oh, but they're just a lot of silly billies. Jeremy Aldrich has been making such calf's eyes at me all afternoon that it was all I could do not to slap him. And all the other gentlemen seem to want to do much the same. But I don't need to worry about that with you, Max. You're much too sophisticated to play those games with me."

"Good God, you think I will not flirt with you as much as any other fellow?"

She laughed. "I am certain you will. You always do. But you do not mean it, not with me. I know you still think me a little country mouse."

"I do not."

"Yes, you do. And that's why I want to waltz with you first. You realize I *am* a country mouse and will teach me all I need to know."

The sensuous curve of her lips lent a more provocative meaning to her words. Could she truly be innocent of their suggestive double meaning? No, Fellowes and Vaughn must have been right, after all. The woman was a coquette. "I am at your service, Miss Lacey." He lowered his voice to the seductive whisper that had brought countless women into his arms. "In *any* capacity whatsoever, I shall be happy to teach you all you need to know."

Was that a blush coloring her cheeks? "Rogue," she said.

"Minx," he replied.

Lord, she made his head spin. Temptress or innocent? Would he ever know the truth?

Chapter 6

When Violet came in to open the draperie, the morning sun struck Rosie in the face like a thunderbolt. She tried to sit up, but the pain was excruciating.

The headaches were back.

Heavens, she must have sunk so low in dissipation that she had quite forgot about her condition. It was odd, but she had experienced none of the debilitating headaches since she'd arrived in London. Please God, don't let them flare up now, just when she was really enjoying herself for the first time in her life.

She sent Violet away with a flick of her hand. No one at home, not even Violet, knew she had contracted her mother's disease. Rosie did not want Violet to see her until she had managed to control the pain.

She began the slow calming exercise she had taught herself in order to get through the dizzy disorientation that always came with the pain. Breathe in. Breathe out. Concentrate on the toes, relaxing each one. Then the foot, then the ankle, then the calf, all the way up her body, one part at a time, until reaching the head. By the time she got to the head, the worst of the pain was usually gone, but the aftereffects of nausea, fatigue, and dizziness lingered sometimes for hours.

This time seemed different somehow. She could not

put her finger on it, but this morning's attack was slightly different from the others. Perhaps it was simply an evolution of the disease. But if so, why did it appear to be less potent, less debilitating? Was her body simply adapting?

Rosie proceeded with her calming exercise, and as she lay there quietly, the pain eased away until she felt perfectly relaxed. Going slowly, as she always did, she pushed herself to a sitting position.

She gasped aloud at the explosion of pain. Even the slightest movement, tilting her face in one direction and then another, made her brain feel like thick liquid sloshing around inside her skull.

This was certainly different. She'd never had this type of headache before.

Rosie eased herself slowly, to the edge of the bed. She swung her legs over and sat immobile for a few moments while her brain slid back into place. Just when she thought she might be able to manage after all, a door slammed somewhere in the house, and seemed to echo inside her head like a carillon.

When Violet entered again sometime later, she found her Mistress still seated on the edge of the bed, her head in her hands.

"Miss? Are you all right?"

The girl's voice resounded in Rosie's ears like the crash of a thousand cymbals. She groaned aloud. "I need tea," she murmured, barely able to speak. "And send my aunt to me, please." It was time to enlist Fanny's help.

By the time her aunt arrived, Rosie had been able to make her way to the chaise near the fire. In the past, the headache had been accompanied by chills, but not this morning. In fact, she found the room to be rather warm. She fanned her face with a theater bill that had been left on the candlestand near the chaise.

Fanny entered the bed chamber wearing a pink silk dressing gown and lace cap. Clearly, she had come straight from her own bed. She took one look at Rosie, clucked her tongue, and perched herself on the edge of the chaise.

"My dear girl," she said, and took one of Rosie's hands between her own, "you look quite done in. I suppose the theater, two routs, and a card party were too much for one evening."

The strong tea had done some good, but even so, Fanny's voice reverberated painfully inside Rosie's head. She lifted a hand to her temple.

"Oh my," Fanny said, lowering her voice as though she knew exactly how Rosie felt. "You really are in a bad way, are you not? Quite a head this morning, eh? Well, I know just the remedy for you. I shall have Mrs. Coolidge make up one of her special morning-after brews. It will have you feeling more the thing in no time at all, I promise."

"I thank you, aunt, but I fear I should see a physician."

Fanny chuckled softly. "Trust me, my dear, this will pass. A little too much champagne—"

"No, it is not that. I—I cannot speak of it just now, but I really must see a physician." Rosie had intended to find a physician in London, one in whom she would confide her condition with a strict promise of confidentiality. She had thought it best to have someone aware of her disease, in case she became really sick or certain medications became necessary. But she had been enjoying herself so much, she had almost completely forgot that she was ill. In fact, until this morning, she had felt perfectly well.

Fanny lifted a hand to Rosie's cheek. "Rosalind, my dear, if something is wrong you must tell me. I will help you in any way you need. Are you ill?"

Rosie sighed. "Yes. But you must not ask me any

more questions, aunt. If you will just be so good as to send for a physician, I would be much obliged to you."

"All right, my dear, it shall be as you wish," Fanny said, her voice gentle and her brow furrowed in concern. "I have no desire to pry, only to let you know you may confide in me at any time. You must know I would respect any confidence. I have grown quite surprisingly fond of you."

"Thank you," Rosie said. Feeling uncharacteristically emotional at her aunt's words, her voice came out watery and weak. She took a deep breath to compose herself. She had no desire to fall apart in front of her aunt. "If there is something you must know," she said with more control, "I promise I will tell you."

"Good. Then I will have Sir Nigel Leighton sent for. He is the best man in London."

Violet helped Rosie to wash up and put on a simple morning dress before the doctor arrived. She could stomach no more than tea and toast when breakfast was offered. Violet's constant fussing, however well-meaning, became irritating and Rosie finally sent the maid away.

When Sir Nigel arrived, Fanny brought him up herself. She introduced them, then made a discreet exit, leaving them alone in the bedchamber. Sir Nigel pulled a finely carved arm chair close to Rosie's chaise and sat down.

"What can I do for you, Miss Lacey?"

The physician was short and stout, with a magnificent head of silver hair. His direct gaze and authoritative air made Rosie feel suddenly foolish and tongue-tied.

"I don't know where to begin," she said.

"At the beginning, I think."

"Well, it all began with my mother."

Sir Nigel lifted a brow. "Go on."

"Before I do," Rosie said, "I must have your word that what I tell you will be kept in the strictest confidence. Even my aunt—especially my aunt—must not know what I am about to tell you."

"You have my word of honor. Now, tell me what troubles you."

And she did. She told him the same things she had told the Exeter physician who'd diagnosed her. She told him how, when Rosie was fourteen, her mother had suddenly become ill, and that in six months she was dead. Now Rosie found herself with the same symptoms. Another physician had confirmed the diagnosis, and predicted Rosie, too, would succumb within six months.

"Tell me more about your mother's illness," Sir Nigel said, and pulled out a small notebook from his waistcoat pocket. "What precisely were her symptoms?"

"I wasn't told everything, of course, but I do know that she suffered horrible headaches. She could always tell they were coming on because her hands and feet became cold. Sometimes she became disoriented and dizzy. When that happened, her nurse or my father bustled her away at once, and we sometimes did not see her for days. My father would come out of her bedchamber looking white-faced and drained, but he never told us what happened behind that closed door. He would simply say that Mama was ill and we must be very quiet and leave her alone."

She waited while he made some notes. He wore an uncompromising scowl and Rosie knew he was not pleased with what she told him. She had been accustomed to their gentle family physician back home. There was nothing gentle, nor even compassionate, about this man. He looked up and asked, "Did these symptoms appear suddenly, or had you ever noticed anything similar when you were younger?"

"Oh, no. It was quite sudden. I remember it well.

She had been out for a ride. When she returned, she was removing her hat and gloves in the hall, and she fainted."

"And then the headaches began," Sir Nigel said. it was not a question. "Did they become more frequent?"

"Yes. And then one day, six months later, Papa came out of her bedchamber looking more devastated than ever, and told us she had died."

"Had a physician attended her during that six months?"

"Yes, Dr. Urquhart."

"A competent man, this Urquhart?" he asked, and made a note. Blast. She ought not to have mentioned the doctor's name. "Well?" he prompted with obvious impatience.

"Yes, I believe he is considered quite competent."

"And no one, your father or Dr. Urquhart or anyone else, ever told you what exactly ailed your mother? Her disease or condition was never named?"

"No. Papa said we were never to speak of it."

"Why?"

"I do not know. I suppose because it was too painful for him. He loved her very much, you see. A dozen years later, he still grieves for her."

He clucked his tongue, though Rosie did not believe it was out of sympathy. He fixed her with his formidable gaze, brows knotted together so tightly they formed deep ridges down the center of his forehead. "And what of you, Miss Lacey? What were your first symptoms and when did they begin?"

"About two months ago," she replied. "I was walking in our park when I suddenly became dizzy and had to sit down. I thought I might faint."

"Did you?"

"No, but the dizziness was quite strong. And then my head began to throb like never before, and my vision became fuzzy."

"What happened next?"

"After a few minutes, the dizziness passed and I was able to make it home safely. I went straight to bed and thought nothing of it. Until two days later, it happened again. This time, I noticed that my hands were freezing, even though I wore gloves. That is what made me think of Mama."

She paused as the recollection of that first moment of panic almost overwhelmed her anew. "Go on," Sir Nigel said, without looking up from his note-taking.

"I kept experiencing the headaches, the dizziness, the cold hands, as well as a ringing in my ears. It was just like Mama. I became scared."

"Did you go to Dr. Urquhart?"

"No."

He looked up. "Why not?"

"I cannot explain it, but I didn't want anyone to know. If my family knew I had Mama's disease, they would know I was going to die. I did not want them to know that. I could not bear it."

"But you said a doctor had confirmed the diagnosis?"

"Yes. I decided I had to know for sure, but I could not go to Dr. Urquhart, who would feel obliged to tell my father. So I went to Exeter one day with my sisters. I told them I wanted to visit the lending library while they shopped. Instead, I went to see a physician, using a different name."

Sir Nigel's mouth puckered with disdain. "And what did he say?"

"He said I had the same disease as my mother."

"But he did not name the disease?"

"No."

He dropped his notebook onto his lap and glared at Rosie with undisguised contempt. "And what did you want of me, Miss Lacey? A more positive diagnosis? I assure you I have not achieved this level of my profession by telling people what they want to know rather than what they need to know."

"Oh no, sir," she said, surprised he would think such a thing. "No, I am quite certain of the diagnosis. I wanted to see you simply to have a physician in London aware of my condition. You see, the headaches have begun again."

"What do you mean, begun again? They stopped?"

"Yes. Since I've been in London these last few weeks, I've had no headache until today."

"And you experienced the same symptoms this morning?"

"Yes. Well, sort of."

"Sort of?"

"It . . . it was not exactly the same this time."

"Was there dizziness?"

"Yes."

"Disorientation?"

"Yes."

"Blurred vision."

"No."

"Coldness in your extremities?"

"No."

"Ringing in your ears?"

"Sort of, though not the same as before. Every sound seemed to echo in my head like a Chinese gong."

"And how do you feel now?"

"Much better, thank you."

"The headache has passed?"

"For the most part."

Sir Nigel rose to his feet and began to pace. He massaged the bridge of his nose with a thumb and forefinger, as though he, too, suffered the headache. "Miss Lacey, your story confounds me. You say you have your mother's disease, yet you have no idea what that disease is. Based on a few very common symptoms, I cannot help but believe you are making a gross assumption of fatality."

"You did not see my mother, Sir Nigel. I tell you, I have exactly the condition she had."

He stopped pacing, turned, and skewered her to the spot with his steely glare. "You will, I trust, allow me a tad more expertise in this area, Miss Lacey. You develop symptoms and do not tell the one doctor who might be able to help you, who treated your mother's illness. You visit another doctor, quite unknown to you, who confirms your own diagnosis, without even knowing what he is diagnosing. I suggest to you, Miss Lacey that no physician worthy of his profession would confirm an unknown diagnosis. I promise you I will not, if that's what you had hoped."

"I do not need your confirmation, Sir Nigel," Rosie said, exasperated at the man's arrogance. Just because he did not make the diagnosis, he found it suspect. The pompous ass! "No, sir, I thought only that you might perhaps prescribe something to relieve the headache, when it comes again. I cannot avoid death, it seems, but I should like to be as comfortable as possible in the meantime."

"You've been in London how long?"

"Almost three weeks."

"And this is the first occurrence of the headache?"

"Yes."

"What did you do last evening, Miss Lacey?"

"I beg your pardon?"

"Did you go out last evening?"

"Yes. "

"To several parties, I daresay."

"Yes. And the theater."

"The theater, too. How nice. And did you have anything to drink at these parties?"

"Yes." Rosie could see where this was heading and she did not like it one bit.

"What did you drink, Miss Lacey?"

"I do not believe it signifies—"

"What did you have to drink?" His tone brooked no equivocation.

"Champagne."

"Quite a lot of it, I would wager."

Rosie shrugged and would not dignify his implication with a direct answer. The truth was she *had* consumed a substantial amount of champagne. But it had tasted so very good.

"Miss Lacey," Sir Nigel said through clenched teeth, "you have wasted my time. The symptoms you have described to me are exactly what one might expect after a night of too much champagne. That is the source of your headache, not some mysterious disease."

"That's as may be, Sir Nigel. I admit I am not accustomed to champagne. But that does not mean that I do not also suffer severe pain due to my condition. I am not one of your swooning, vaporish females, I promise you. I do not feign illness to draw attention to myself. Quite the contrary. I *do* suffer from my mother's disease. Of that I am quite, quite certain."

"You may be right," he said. "You may indeed have contracted a fatal condition, one that is perhaps hereditary. However, I have too little information to go on. And despite my professional instinct that this is mere foolishness, I confess I am intrigued. Your mother's case was real enough, and that interests me. I should like to contact this Dr. Urquhart and get all the medical details of your mother's illness."

"No!"

He gave her another one of those flinty looks that surely intimidated all his other patients into doing exactly what he asked. "I promise not to mention your name, if you insist on this ridiculous secrecy, Miss Lacey. I shall simply tell him I have a patient who is related to the late Lady Lacey and suspects she may have the same disease. I will ask for your mother's history so I may be more precise in my own diagnosis."

"I don't know. I don't want—"

"I *promise*. No names. And when I hear back from him, I will let you know what I have discovered."

Rosie gave a deep sigh. She could tell the man was not going to give up. "All right. But I will have your pledge of confidentiality."

"Have I not given it, Miss Lacey? More than once? Now, I will have the direction of Dr. Urquhart, if you please."

Chapter 7

"Why the frown, Fanny? Do not tell me your charge has done something to displease you?"

Max had just arrived, admittedly late, at Almack's. Mr. Willis was ready to close the doors when Max had bounded through the entrance. He had been in the midst of an extraordinary winning streak at Brooks's and had been loathe to depart. It was only his promise to dance with Rosalind that prevented him from playing on into the wee hours.

If truth be told, it was not an entirely honorable commitment to a promise. He wanted to waltz with Rosalind, and not because he was obliged to do so. Max could hardly wait to take the girl in his arms and glide her through the dance, to hold her close, to feel her waist beneath his hand, to breathe in her scent, to gaze down into her flashing eyes.

He could not believe he was having such thoughts about an innocent rustic. She was not his style at all, but had somehow got under his skin. He must attempt to keep these foolish impulses under control. Despite her years, Rosalind was a green girl. She was not for him.

He had noticed her the moment he'd entered the room: a vision in scarlet among the white-clad debutantes. Max wondered if it was Fanny's doing that saw her niece so frequently in shades of red, or if the girl wore it simply to shock. No matter. She looked

best in red. It suited her coloring and her unquench-
able high spirits.

Rosalind's spirits appeared particularly high tonight
as she danced the quadrille with Rodney Oswald-
Jones.

Max looked back at Fanny, who still frowned.
"Fanny? What has the minx done?"

"Nothing at all," she said, schooling her features
into a smile that did not reach her eyes.

A tall, gray-haired gentlemen stepped up behind
Fanny and said, "She is not displeased with Rosalind.
She is concerned. Good evening, my dear." Lord Eldridge brought Fanny's gloved fingers to his lips. Max
wondered when Fanny would put the besotted man
out of his misery and marry him.

"Hush, Jonathan," Fanny said in an undertone, and
directed her eyes toward the dance floor.

Max followed her gaze. "Egad, Fanny, do not tell
me you are worried about that fatuous tulip, Oswald-
Jones?" he asked. "The man's safe as milk."

"I have no objection to the young man," Fanny
said, "except perhaps for that peacock-blue waistcoat
with the lavender embroidery. What could he have
been thinking? Do you suppose he merely seeks attention, or does he truly believe the thing is remotely
acceptable?"

"Do not try to fob me off with non sequiturs, my
dear," Max said. "Eldridge says you are concerned.
What has happened?"

Fanny shot a look of displeasure toward Lord Eldridge, but then gave a resigned sigh. "I am sure it
is nothing," she said. "And I am also sure Rosalind
will not appreciate my telling you. Or you either,
Jonathan. So I will trust both of you to keep this matter to yourselves."

"Of course, Fanny." Max experienced a moment of
apprehension that Rosalind had, as he'd predicted,

landed herself into some kind of trouble. For some inexplicable reason, the notion did not sit well with him.

"If you must know," Fanny said, "I am concerned for the girl's health."

"Her health?" Max looked across the floor at the dazzling figure of Rosalind, gracefully but energetically stepping through the dance, pure enjoyment radiating from the smile on her face. Her health was the last thing he would expect her aunt, or anyone else, to be concerned about.

"She spent almost an hour this morning with Sir Nigel Leighton," Fanny said.

Her words brought Max up short. "Leighton?" Good Lord, it must be something serious. The man was physician to most of the London aristocracy, but was especially noted for his no-nonsense, somewhat dispassionate approach to medicine. He did not suffer fools, and had been known to walk out on those who wasted his time on self-indulgent nervous conditions. He would not have spent an hour on a trifling case of the vapors.

"Why did he come?" Max asked. "She looks perfectly fit to me."

"She asked for a doctor," Fanny said. "She would not tell me why."

How curious. The girl must have a secret. All sorts of interesting possibilities leapt to mind. "What did Leighton say when he left?"

"Nothing," Fanny said, almost spitting out the word in disgust. "He would not tell me anything, save to remind me in no uncertain terms that what was said between a doctor and his patient was private. Controlling my urge to strike the impudent man, I asked for a simple reassurance that Rosalind was not unwell. As her aunt, I felt I had the right to know of anything serious. But all he would say was that I should not worry. How can I not worry? If nothing were amiss, why did he spend so long with her?"

Max's imagination spun off into all sorts of directions, most of them less than respectable, some downright scandalous. But if Rosalind was in that sort of trouble, it was unlikely to have happened in London. She'd only been here a few weeks. Was she not, after all, the innocent he believed her to be?

"You have grown fond of the girl, my dear," Eldridge said. "It is only natural to be concerned. But I cannot believe Leighton would not at least have given you a hint if there was something seriously wrong."

"I agree," Max said, thinking it best not to dwell on the topic. "If the most respected physician in London says not to worry, then I shouldn't worry. I declare, Fanny, you have become a veritable mother hen."

"Hateful boy! I am nobody's hen and I'll thank you to remember that. I am fond of Rosalind. That is all."

"Just so," Eldridge agreed.

"She is so different from what I expected," Fanny said, "so vibrant, so alive, so eager to do everything."

"Which includes flaunting propriety at every opportunity," Max said.

"I know!" Fanny's eyes twinkled with amusement. "Is it not delicious? What do you suppose Edmund will say when he discovers his eldest daughter has become the talk of the town?"

"You are a bad woman," Max said. "Eldridge, what are we to do with her? She is hoping for trouble."

"If I know Fanny," Eldridge said, and winked at her, "she is merely looking for a bit of spice to flavor a dull Season."

"You are quite right, Jonathan, darling," she said. "Besides, I like her. I enjoy her. In fact, I cannot recall when I have so enjoyed a Season. She has more life in her than I would ever have expected from any of Edmund's brood."

"She's too lively by half," Max said, grinning. "And so irrepressibly high-spirited, she makes one's head spin. She's up to anything, I'll give her that. Intrepid as they come. You ought to have seen her driving Aldrich's team the other day. What a stir she caused!"

"So I heard." Fanny beamed with such pride it was all Max could do not to burst out laughing. Mother hen, indeed.

"And you are right," he went on, "she wants to do absolutely everything, or so she says. I tell you, she quite exhausts me just listening to all her plans."

"I know," Fanny said. "She has a list."

"Does she? Next you will tell me she has a guide-book as well."

"She bought a copy of *The Picture of London* the day after she arrived."

"Egad!" Max gave a shudder. "How horribly quaint." He reconsidered his interesting speculations based on Leighton's visit. He could not reconcile the idea of a fast sophisticate with someone who came to London with a pokey little guidebook and a list of things to do.

The quadrille had ended and Rosalind stood surrounded by an impressive company of swains. She had a smile, a word, a laugh for each one of them, and they buzzed about her like bees seeking nectar. Damn, but the woman confounded him. Truly, he could not decide if she was an innocent rustic stretching her wings, or a practiced flirt. Or, paradoxically, a bit of both?

Max turned his back to the vulgar spectacle in time to see several plumed and jeweled matrons glaring indignantly in Rosalind's direction. Stealing their charges' beaux again, he supposed, and putting all their insipid little charges in the shade with her bold red ensemble. He could hardly blame the gentlemen.

Rosalind was something new, something different. Whereas most of Society preferred an appearance of ennui, a total indifference to everything and everyone—an attitude Max himself had honed to perfection—Rosalind was unashamed in her excitement, her enthusiasm, her amusement, her gaiety. The pure joy of life glowed in her eyes and her radiant smile and her unreserved laughter.

Max had never known anyone quite like Rosalind Lacey. And neither had any of the other men clustered about her.

"Rosalind may be a grown woman," Fanny said, "but perhaps I really ought to keep a closer eye on her after all. She does seem to attract all sorts, does she not?"

"Indeed," Max said.

"Why, even Overton has entered her circle. I would not have thought her his type, but—"

"What?" Max spun around to see Lord Overton kissing Rosalind's outstretched hand. The man was a notorious libertine with the face of an Adonis. He was a devil, a cad, a blackguard of the first degree. Yet no woman seemed immune to his charm. Max could not bear to think of his innocent Rosalind succumbing to the man's oily seduction.

"I believe it is time for my waltz," he said, and hurried to the bandstand where he slipped the orchestra leader a five-pound note to change the order of tunes.

"Did I not tell you, Jonathan?" Fanny said when Max was out of earshot. She tried without success to suppress a grin. "The boy is smitten."

"You provoked him."

"I did no such thing. I simply mentioned Overton."

"Overton," Lord Eldridge said, "the only man in

town ever to best Davenant. Stole Lady Fallon right
from under his nose."

"Yes, poor Max did not fare well in that little es-
capade. He's never forgiven Overton. But his blond
lordship is a formidable rival: devilishly handsome,
charming, a clever seducer. If you want my opinion,
the entire episode did Max a world of good. A taste
of failure now and again builds character. Max was
becoming too sure of himself. Too complacent. Bored
with the game."

"Davenant is always bored."

Fanny smiled as she watched her young friend talking with the orchestra leader, exerting himself to a degree she had not seen in years. "Not any more."

Rosie could barely concentrate on all the gentlemen surrounding her, though they offered compliments and flattery enough to swell her head to
bursting. Ever since she had seen Max Davenant arrive, she could think of nothing but that waltz he'd
promised.

She had thought he wasn't coming and could barely
contain her disappointment. The morning's headache
and Sir Nigel's visit served to remind her of how little time she had left. She must not waste another moment. With every intention of making this evening
especially memorable, Rosie had taken extra care to
look her best tonight. She wore her favorite dress of
crimson silk over a darker red satin slip edged in pink
tulle quilling. A fillet of tiny pink blossoms had been
woven through her short curls, and she even wore
new pink kid slippers.

She had begun to believe her efforts had been
wasted. The orchestra had already played one waltz,
and Rosie had been tempted to dance it with someone else, though she would have been disappointed
to do so. For some reason, she had got hold of the

notion that she must dance the first waltz with Max
and no one else. She had even dreamed about it the
night before, about twirling around an empty dance
floor in Max's arms, his liquid brown eyes smiling
down into hers. But when hours went by without his
making an appearance, Rosie had begun to consider
another partner.

As it happened, she was spared the decision, for
no one had asked her to waltz. The gentlemen of the
ton seemed determined to honor the silly Almack's
rule. It was a mystery how they knew she had not
been granted the precious permission to waltz, but it
appeared to be generally understood. So she had sat
out the first waltz with Fanny and watched with envy
as other couples twirled about the floor.

When she had sighed aloud, Lady Teresa Carmichael,
seated in the next chair, smiled and said she wished
she could waltz, too. A shy young girl in her first Season, Lady Teresa was a pattern card of propriety. "But
I shall not receive permission until I have been presented."

"I have no intention of waiting for someone's permission," Rosie had replied. "If I had been asked, I
assure you I would be waltzing this minute."

"You would waltz without permission?" Lady
Teresa's eyes grew wide as saucers, as though Rosie
had admitted to treason.

"Of course I would. So should you, and anyone
else who wishes to waltz. I cannot believe a handful
of top-lofty ladies can tell all of Society what to do.
It is absurd."

"I am afraid I would not have the courage to defy
the rules," Lady Teresa said.

"Well, I am not afraid to do so."

"You are braver than I, Miss Lacey. Braver than
anyone, I daresay. But if you were to waltz, would
you not be afraid people would think you fast?"

"Oh, but I intend to be fast," Rosie replied. "I have so much to do in so short a time, I cannot afford to be slow about it."

Lady Teresa gave her a quizzical look, but Rosie had been too wrapped up in her disappointment and did not elaborate.

Max was here now, though, and he would not forget his promise. Rosie would have her waltz.

"—beautiful in red," Lord Overton was saying. She really must pay attention. As Fanny always said, a lady should never take a gentleman's flattery for granted.

"You are too kind, my lord," she said, gazing directly into the man's deep blue eyes. Heavens, but he was handsome. He was beautifully dressed in the darkest blue jacket, setting off his fair hair and eyes, a waistcoat of white satin embroidered with tiny blue and gray flowers, and gray satin breeches. She had been immediately captivated by his good looks and irresistible charm when he had forced Mr. Newcombe into an introduction and before she had been distracted by the sight of Max walking toward the bandstand.

"I am prepared to be much kinder, given the opportunity." Lord Overton's husky croon told Rosie he was a rake of the highest order. Like Max. He had a voice not unlike Max's in its seductive qualities, but his gaze was more disconcerting. Whereas she found only a playful flirtation in Max's eyes, this man looked at her in such a way that made her believe he had more than flirtation in mind. Much more. And it made her uncomfortable.

She could not have said why, but Rosie was fairly certain that if Max had looked at her in that way, she would not have minded half as much, even though he was every bit as much a rake as Lord Overton.

"I would be charmed beyond measure," Lord Overton said, "if you would grant me the pleasure of the next dance."

"Sorry, old chap. I'm afraid Miss Lacey promised the next dance to me."

A thrill coursed through Rosie's veins at the sound of Max's voice. She was going to have her waltz now!

"I did not see you arrive, Davenant," Lord Overton said. "But I do believe I have the advantage of you here. Again. You see, I asked Miss Lacey first."

"Ah, but we have a long-standing commitment, Miss Lacey and I. Do we not, my dear?"

Rosie grinned to think that two rakes were actually vying for her company. How perfectly delightful. "We do," she said. "I am sorry, Lord Overton, but I have indeed promised this dance to Mr. Davenant. Perhaps another time?"

She took Max's arm and had literally to bite her tongue to keep from shrieking with excitement as the orchestra struck up the opening strains of a waltz, and Max led her onto the dance floor. It was not merely the notion of waltzing that had her all aflutter. It was waltzing with Max.

Why was it none of the other gentlemen who led her out to dance had caused such a tremor of anticipation to skitter up and down her spine? Other men, especially Lord Overton, were equally handsome. Others were as witty. All of them flirted and flattered and made her feel special. There was something about Max, however, that set him apart from the rest. Whereas Lord Overton made her uneasy, she felt perfectly comfortable with Max. Though he was a rake and a gambler and could seduce a girl with the lift of an eyebrow, Rosie felt safe with him. Deep down, she believed him to be a true gentleman, that his rakish notoriety and perpetual ennui were nothing more than a pose.

And Rosie knew all about poses. Was she not masquerading as the bold and sophisticated Rosalind when beneath it all she was still plain, simple Rosie Lacey of Wycombe Hall who could hardly believe she did the things she did and said the things she said?

As they took their place in the center of the floor, Rosie heard a sharp gasp and looked up to see an attractive woman, who wore a ridiculous number of green plumes, scowling and whispering to the woman next to her. She might as well have pointed her finger directly at Rosie, she was so obviously speaking of her. "Who is that odious woman, Max?"

"That, my dear minx, is Mrs. Drummond-Burrell. The woman beside her is Lady Castlereagh. They are two of the patronesses."

"You mean the ones whose permission I am supposed to plead before dancing the waltz? How marvelous! They shall see how much I care for their beastly rules. Let us dance."

Max placed his left hand at Rosie's waist and held out his right hand. "Place your right hand in mine and your left on my shoulder."

"Oh, I know how it is done. I have watched and watched. Lead on, Max!"

With the merest pressure at her waist, he led her into the dance. It was easy to follow the rhythm of the music as well as Max's gentle yet persuasive lead. In less than a moment, Rosie found herself twirling and spinning in perfect accord with the music. It was pure heaven.

Max had her completely in his control. She kept her eyes on his, and everything else seemed to fade away. There was only Max, with his intense brown eyes and soft smile, the hand at her waist pressing so gently it might have been a caress. She closed her eyes, drinking in the scent of him—bay rum, brandy, the starch of his neckcloth—and let the music, and Max, guide her steps.

For this moment alone, the trip to London had been worthwhile.

"You dance well, minx." Rosie opened her eyes to find him gazing down at her, a smile tugging at one corner of his mouth. "Are you enjoying your first waltz?"

"Oh yes, Max, very much. It is truly magical. How kind of you to lead me out. You dance quite well yourself."

Amusement sparkled in his eyes. "I wonder whether you enjoy the dancing so much as you enjoy the uproar."

"Uproar?" Rosie reluctanly tore her gaze from his and glanced about the room. Several groups had gathered together—women, mostly—all of them whispering and glaring at Rosie and Max with outraged disapproval. One woman leaned heavily against another, fanning herself vigorously as though about to swoon. "Are all these people upset because a little nobody from the country dares to ignore their silly rules?"

"Apparently."

"Hmph. What a lot of fuss over nothing."

"Nothing? I could have sworn that only a moment ago you were quite enjoying the dance."

"Oh, but I am. I am indeed. We shall pay no attention to those spineless ninnies who allow others to dictate their behavior. This is much too splendid to worry about such nonsense. Even more splendid than I had hoped. Just dance with me, Max."

"Is waltzing on your list?"

She looked up at him sharply. "How do you know about my list?"

"Your aunt mentioned it. Fanny believes it only includes such innocuous entries as visiting the Tower or Westminster Abbey. But I suspect there are *other* sorts of activities on that list." A slow, lazy grin split his face, and he winked at her.

Rosie threw back her head and laughed. "And what of it?" she asked.

"I merely wondered if I was helping to check off one of the entries. I assume you are dutifully checking them off as you go?"

"Rogue! I shall always be the country mouse to you. But if you must know, by the end of this evening, I believe I shall have checked off several items on my list." For one thing, she was determined to be thoroughly kissed. Rosie did not believe Max would accommodate her there. He did not think of her in that way. She was no more than an amusing rustic, a mere diversion. Max was used to glamorous high flyers and only flirted with her out of mischief, or out of habit, or possibly because Fanny asked him to do so. In any case, it meant nothing. Rosie was quite certain, however, she could entice one of the other gentlemen into kissing her. Lord Radcliffe, perhaps?

"Such as?"

"I beg your pardon?"

"You were woolgathering, minx. I asked what sort of items on your list will get checked off tonight?"

"Oh. Well, besides this waltz—you were correct, it is on my list—I have engaged in a flirtation with a full-fledged rake. Lord Overton."

She had, of course, checked off that item some time ago, but she would not give Max the pleasure of knowing he had helped her do so.

His brows rose in surprise. "And what am I, pray tell?"

"Practically family."

He rolled his eyes toward the ceiling. "You delight in throwing those words back at me, do you not? I'll have you know I can flirt circles around Overton."

"Oh? Show me."

"Well, now you have put me on the spot, minx."

"Show me."

"All right, then. I suppose Overton filled your head with compliments? Give me an example, if you please."

"He said I looked beautiful in red."

"Just like that? 'You look beautiful in red?'"

"I believe that was how he said it."

"Amateur. The man has no finesse."

"Are you saying I do not look beautiful in red?"

"Quite the contrary, my minx. But if I were going to seriously flirt with you, I would tell you how the crimson of your gown merely reflects the vitality of your spirit, a vitality that burns like a blazing fire to singe a man's soul."

"Oh."

"But I would not stop there." His voice dropped to a husky whisper so low Rosie had to lean closer to catch every word. "I would tell you how the soft red silk enhances the natural flush of your perfectly sculpted cheeks—cheeks softer even than the silk, petal-soft, beckoning one to touch, to stroke, to caress. And how the fiery color echoes the tantalizing hints of auburn caught by the candlelight in your glorious hair—thick, luxurious hair such as a man craves to run his fingers through. And how the deep red hue is reminiscent of the damask rose, though its fragrance is no match for the intoxicating scent of you, a scent that takes a man's breath away and makes him want to bury his face against your long white neck and breathe deeply of it. And how the rich color emulates the sweet tint of your lips—full, lush, sensual lips ripe for a man to kiss, very gently, very softly, tasting, exploring, savoring, and finally devouring with the full force of his desire. Yes, you look very beautiful in red, minx."

"Oh, my." The room had suddenly grown quite warm.

"Do they not make a splendid couple, Jonathan?"

"They make a splendid scandal," he replied. "Only

see how that devil is holding her too close. By Jove, it looks as if he means to kiss her, right here in public. And look how everyone is tittering and gaping. You ought to have known what would happen, Fanny. Rosalind's reputation will be in tatters. Doors will close in her face. She will endure cut after cut."

"Then it is well I am here to guide her," Fanny said, "for I know a thing or two about being cut. Besides, darling, the girl is irrepressible. Do you think I can stop her from doing anything she pleases?"

"Possibly not. It seems a shame, though. I like her, Fanny."

"So do I." Fanny smiled wistfully. "She so much reminds me of myself when I was young."

She watched her niece, as did everyone else in the room, gazing dreamily up at Max while he pulled her slightly closer. From the look in Rosalind's eyes, Max must be using all his considerable wiles upon her, filling her head with outrageous flattery and sweet lies. And barely a breath away from kissing her. Incorrigible boy!

Would it not be lovely, she thought, if Rosalind and Max became lovers? Just like Fanny and Basil Davenant so many years before. If her niece found half the pleasure with Max that Fanny had with Basil, if they fell in love . . . well, she could wish no greater happiness for the girl.

Fanny scanned the room for a friendly face among the scowling high sticklers when her gaze fell upon a vaguely familiar and very young man intently watching Max and Rosalind. Her niece had won another admirer, she thought, but then full recognition dawned.

"By God, it is young Thomas Lacey!"

"What's that?" Lord Eldridge asked.

"Rosalind's eldest brother. The tall, thin young fellow in the bottle-green coat, just over there." Fanny chuckled at the wide-eyed incredulity on the boy's face. What must he think of his once shy and dowdy older sister, now fashionable and dancing an almost indecent waltz in arms of an infamous womanizer?

"There'll be the devil to pay now," she said. "He will likely show up at my front door tomorrow, rip up at Rosalind, and report every juicy detail back to his father. Impudent puppy. Perhaps I will have a brief word or two with him."

Just as she made a move to approach Thomas, another young man tugged on his arm and pulled him away. A moment later he had disappeared through the main entrance.

After the waltz, Fanny coaxed Rosalind into leaving. She could not decide whether or not to tell her niece that Lady Jersey had asked that Fanny remove Miss Lacey from the premises, stating that her vouchers would no longer be honored. Fanny was amused at the woman's outrage and was perfectly happy to be barred once again from Almack's doors. It was a sort of badge of honor. Some of the best people had been barred: the Duchess of Bedford, Lady Rochford, Lord Marsdon. She rather suspected Rosalind might also appreciate being among such elite company.

Their next stop was the Easterbrook ball, where news of Rosalind's behavior at Almack's had already spread as the latest *on-dit*. Her niece's popularity among the gentlemen only increased with her new notoriety: every rake, rogue, and libertine sought to partner her. She danced every dance, and Fanny so enjoyed watching her niece conquer Society by defying it, she did not realize until much later that she had forgot all about Thomas Lacey.

Lord William Radcliffe had remained one of Rosalind's most stalwart admirers since their first meeting. They had danced earlier in the evening, and when Fanny saw them stroll through the terrace doors, she could easily guess what the young man had in mind.

"And what makes you smile like the cat who swallowed the canary?"

She thought Max, who had naturally followed them to Easterbrook House, would remain in the card room the rest of the evening, and was surprised to see him back in the ballroom. "It is all your fault, my boy."

"What is my fault?"

"You have led my niece straight into the arms of every libertine in town with that wretched Almack's waltz. Upon my soul, Max, it looked as though you meant to make love to the girl right there on the spot, with all the *ton* looking on and the patronesses swooning."

A smile twitched at the edge of his mouth. "I merely flirted with her. Nothing more."

"Quite so. And now, because no woman can resist such charm, you have made her appear fast, thereby giving permission to every other young buck to have a go at her. Why, only a few moments ago Lord Radcliffe maneuvered her onto the terrace, and I am certain you can imagine his intentions."

"The devil you say."

"Yes. Oh, and here they come now. I ask you, Max, does she not have the look of a woman who has just been well and truly kissed?"

"Well, I'm dashed!"

Fanny gave a smug smile as Max turned on his heels and stalked away like an angry bear. Yes indeed, the boy was definitely smitten.

Chapter 8

Rosie heaped her plate with a most unladylike quantity of food. She was ravenous, having eaten very little the night before. During supper, she and Mr. Newcombe, her partner for the supper dance, had been joined by several other couples, and more talking and laughing had taken place than eating.

There had been no recurrence of the headache this morning, for which she was grateful. One more day, at least, without the disease overtaking her. She sat down at the breakfast table and a footman poured her a cup of tea. When he asked if there was anything else she would like, Rosie looked at her plate and laughed. "No, Thomas, I am persuaded this mountain of food will suffice."

When the footman had left her alone with her meal, Rosie considered some of the other appetites she'd indulged during her stay in London—appetites she hadn't even known existed. The longer she stayed with Fanny, the more she came to realize how much of her life in Devon had been spent as a spectator, watching her siblings' lives unfold but almost never taking part in the action herself. So many wasted years!

She was almost thankful for the dread disease. Without it, she would never have had the courage to do some of things she'd done. In fact, she would have been mortified at her indecorous behavior. However, knowing she had but a few short months left on this earth, she had ceased to care what anyone thought of Rosalind, including the ever reserved and proper Rosie.

With so little time left, she was pleased to have worked her way through so much of her list. She had indeed managed to achieve the two major objectives set for the evening. She had waltzed with Max, and she had been kissed.

When she had agreed to stroll on the terrace with Lord Radcliffe, she knew he meant to kiss her. Of all her admirers, she had hoped it would be him. She liked him. He made her laugh and flirted outrageously. She had been told he had a reputation as an active rake, but nothing quite as wicked as Max or Lord Overton. Just your ordinary, everyday rake.

Rosie smiled to think how low she had sunk to consider a rake as ordinary. What would her sisters, especially Ursula, say if they knew the sort of men with whom their spinster sister consorted?

Last evening, she had most definitely consorted with Lord Radcliffe.

She had wanted more than a simple kiss—she had been kissed before, twice, by young men in the neighborhood near Wycombe Hall. Rosie had wanted to be *thoroughly* kissed, whatever that meant. She had once overheard her sister Pamela telling Ursula how John Stansfield, now Pamela's husband, had thoroughly kissed her the night before. Ursula, ever prim and proper, had shushed her youngest sister before Rosie could hear any more. But the dreamy tone of Pamela's voice told her it had been wonderful.

There was no question that Lord Radcliffe had been thorough, and Rosie had enjoyed it. He had held her very close and had done more than simply press his lips against hers. Much more. Why, then, was she somehow reluctant to check the item off her list, as though the kiss had been less than satisfactory?

"Heavens, child, are you going to eat all that?" Fanny swept into the breakfast room and took a seat opposite Rosie. Her aunt seldom joined her for breakfast, and Rosie wondered what brought her downstairs so early this morning.

The footman had followed Fanny into the room and proceeded to serve her tea, bread, and jam from the sideboard. She looked across at Rosie's plate and grimaced. "Do you eat like this every morning? I do not know how you do it."

"I am not usually so piggish, aunt, I assure you. But I am especially hungry this morning." Rosie grinned sheepishly. "And I did not think anyone would be witness to my gluttony."

"Caught out!" Fanny said. "How you stay so slender on such a diet is a mystery to me."

"What brings you down so early?"

"I wished to have a word with you. I forgot to mention it last night. It just flew right out of my head."

"What did?"

"Who, not what. Thomas. I saw Thomas at Almack's."

"Thomas?" Rosie looked around for the footman of that name. Surely *he* had not been at Almack's.

"Your brother, my dear. He was watching you waltz with Max."

Rosie almost choked on her eggs as a knot formed in the pit of her stomach. "Thomas? Here in London?" Her brother had been on a walking tour of the Lake District with two of his friends from Cambridge. What was he doing in London? She had been so certain none of her family would be in town during her visit— no one to see her new mode of dress, her indiscreet behavior, her curricle racing, her flirting, her waltzing, her kissing rakes. But now Thomas had seen. "Oh, God."

"Yes, I thought you might not be pleased. I fully

expect the boy to turn up on my doorstep this morning and demand to take you home to Edmund."

"No!" Not yet. She was not ready to go home yet. There was still so much she wanted to do. She would not allow her brother to spoil what time was left to her. "No, he will not," she said with conviction. "I am of age—four years his senior in fact. He cannot tell me what to do."

"That's the spirit!"

"If he comes, I shall be happy to see him. But if he kicks up a ruckus over what he saw last night, I shall send *him* packing. But truly, aunt, Thomas has never been so very high in the instep. Not like Ursula. I do not believe Thomas will give me away. Did he see anything else? I mean, besides the waltz? Was he at the Easterbrook ball as well?"

"I did not see him there. Were you afraid he might have seen something, for example, like your return from the terrace on Lord Radcliffe's arm with your lips swollen and your cheeks flushed?"

Rosie's hands flew to her cheeks, which were flushing even now. "Oh, no. Please tell me you exaggerate, aunt. Please tell me it was not so obvious."

"Only to those who were looking." Fanny began to chuckle. "Of course, almost everyone *was* looking. After your Almack's waltz with Max—who, by the way, received a good scold from me for looking as though he meant to ravish you on the spot—all eyes were upon you through the rest of the evening, even those that pretended they were not. Word of your little spectacle spread fast, my dear."

"Oh, dear. Did I make a complete cake of myself?"

"On the contrary," Fanny said. "I am persuaded every woman there was green with envy. First, every rake and rogue at Almack's gathers around you, and ignores the crop of young chits trotted out by their mamas. Do not underestimate the irresistible lure of a rake, even for the most sober and respectable of women. They may snort and scowl, but you may depend upon it, each one of them wishes it had been her that attracted the attention of so many interesting men. Then, the most celebrated rake of them all leads you into a waltz during which he dances altogether too close, and with you looking wide-eyed and completely enthralled. What on earth was he saying to put such a look in your eyes?"

Rosie sighed at the recollection of Max's words. "He said I looked beautiful in red."

"Hmph. I suspect he said a great deal more, but never mind. Then, after dancing with every attractive man at the Easterbrook ball, you disappear for a quarter hour with Lord Radcliffe and return looking well kissed, and him looking smug as the cock of the walk. All in all, I would wager you had a better evening than any other woman in the room, and they all knew it."

Rosie could no longer hold back her smile. "It *was* rather wonderful. All of it."

"Tell me about William Radcliffe and his kiss. Was he any good at it?"

A laugh exploded from Rosie like a sneeze. Her aunt's audacious question took her quite by surprise. But if anyone could help her sort out her feelings, it would be this worldly woman with all her experience of men. "I am not sure," Rosie said at last. "He seemed to know what he was about."

"I should think so," Fanny said, eyes alight with amusement. "But your reaction tells me something was lacking."

"I cannot think what it could be," Rosie said. "He did more with his lips and his—" She stopped, feeling suddenly awkward to be speaking of such intimacies.

"His tongue?"

Rosie's cheeks were aflame with embarrassment and she knew she must be glowing bright as a strawberry. "Yes. Let us say simply that he did more than I expected. And yet . . ."

"He did not set your soul on fire? You did not feel your toes curl up in your slippers and your knees grow so weak you would have collapsed had he not been holding you?"

Rosie stared at her aunt. "Is that how it is supposed to be?"

"With the right man. Unfortunately, it sounds as though Lord Radcliffe is not the right man. Pity. He has such lovely golden hair. Well, no matter. You must simply keep looking for him."

"For whom?"

"For the right man, of course."

"But I am not looking for the right man," Rosie said. "I have told you I am not shopping for a husband. I only want to enjoy a few things before—" she almost said before it's too late, but caught herself in time "—before I return to Devon."

"Quite so. And who said anything about husbands? Enjoyment has nothing to do with them. And I do believe, despite the less than perfect kiss, you rather enjoyed yourself last evening."

"Oh, I did. Very much."

"Especially your waltz?"

"Yes, especially that. I am sorry it caused so much talk. I still cannot credit how those odious women are allowed to set the rules for everyone else."

"It was not so much your defiance of their petty rules as the way you and Max danced." A mischievous grin split her face. "My dear, it was almost scandalous. He held you much too close."

"Did he?" Rosie had been aware of little more than his eyes and his voice and the spell he spun with his words. She became warm all over at the memory of it.

"Yes, he did. Because you are older, I think you might have got away with breaking the rules had Max danced with you properly."

"I confess it seemed perfectly proper to me." And perfectly wonderful.

Fanny gave a crack of laughter. "He is a devil, that boy. Knows what to do with a dance."

"Rules or no rules," Rosie said, "I cannot wait to do it again. By the way, Lady Samantha Kirby has arranged a group to attend the Opera House masquerade this week. I told her I would go. I believe she invited Max as well." She was quite sure of it, actually. "And Lord Radcliffe, Alfred Hepworth, Dwight Newcombe, and several others. I hope you do not mind? Are they quite improper, these masquerades?"

"Sometimes. They are frequented by the cits and tradesmen and all sorts from the underclasses. But with everyone masked, one never really knows who is there."

"You do not mind if I go?"

"Of course not, darling. It is sure to be grand fun. I used to attend now and then, years ago."

"What did you wear?"

Fanny chuckled. "All sorts of daring costumes. My favorite was a shepherd, complete with crook and lamb. And short pants. I was a classical shepherd, you see. A sort of Daphnis. My, but it was liberating to dance without the confines of skirts."

"How I should love to do that! Perhaps I can convince you to help me put together an equally shocking costume. But what I should really enjoy, if you will indulge me, is for you to tell me more of your favorite memories. What other shocking things did you do when you were younger?"

"So many things." Fanny gazed into the distance

and smiled. Her blue eyes softened as though recollecting an especially pleasant moment from the past. "So many things. Those were wild and wondrous days."

They sat for some time, nibbling at their breakfast and sipping their tea, while Fanny related tales of her youth. When the footman looked impatient to clear the table, they moved to the morning room. Rosie sat in a large wing chair with her feet tucked beneath her skirts. Fanny snuggled into a corner of the sofa and stretched out her legs. At Rosie's prompting, she continued to tell stories of exotic parties, of yacht races, of dancing naked in fountains, of Paris before the revolution, of risqué theatricals, of champagne baths, of Brighton and the Prince Regent. What a life her aunt had led! How Rosie wished she had not waited until it was almost too late to begin to know this remarkable woman.

"Tell me, aunt, what is the single most precious memory in your life? If you were allowed only one memory to take with you to the grave, what would it be?"

Without hesitation, Fanny said, "Making love with the one man I truly loved, lying in his arms and knowing he loved me, too. That is the greatest memory of all. I would sacrifice all the rest, everything in life, but I would not give up that memory."

The words were spoken with such quiet passion, Rosie could feel the sting of tears building up behind her eyes. She had asked the question in hopes of learning the one perfect thing to be experienced before she died. And now she knew what that was.

Rosie saw that Fanny's eyes glistened with unshed tears of her own. "I am sorry I never knew Uncle Roderick," she said. "It is wonderful that you loved him so much."

Fanny looked up, puzzled. "Parkhurst? Good heavens, my dear, I was not speaking of Parkhurst. I was fond of him, to be sure. But there has been only one true love in my life. Basil Davenant, the Earl of Blythe. Max's father."

"Oh." Rosie had assumed the relationship had been merely one among many, a brief affair, nothing more. She had no idea it had been so important. No wonder Fanny was so fond of Max. He must remind her of Basil. Her one true love. "Why did you never marry him?"

"I was married to Parkhurst when I met Basil. He was married, too, and had four children. But it did not matter. We loved each deeply until the end of his life."

So, the one experience Rosie truly ought to have before she died was to make love with a man. She supposed there were any number of gentlemen willing to take on the task, but she had no idea how to go about it. Inviting a kiss was one thing. This was quite another.

"And so, the greatest experience in your rich and full life was of making love to a man?"

"Not just making love, my dear. One has many lovers throughout one's life, even at my age." She grinned so girlishly Rosie could see how she still attracted a man's attention. "But making love with a man you love deeply and completely and who is madly in love with you . . ." She sighed and a wistful softness gathered in her eyes. "There is nothing to compare with that, my dear."

This might be even more difficult than she'd thought. How was she to get a man to fall madly in love with her? "Are you saying one needs to be in love in order to appreciate the . . . the act of love?"

Fanny gave her a quizzical look. "What are you planning, my girl? Has one of those young men suggested an assignation of some kind?"

"No, aunt. Nothing of the sort, I promise you. I am

merely curious. My mother died when I was a young girl, you know, and I never had a chance to speak with her of such things."

"Ah. Well, then, to answer your question, no, it is not at all necessary to be in love to enjoy sex. One must open up oneself to all life has to offer. Physical pleasure is one of our greatest gifts and I believe one should take advantage of every opportunity to partake of it. But when one is in love, ah, that is something else. More than merely physical. That is what I meant, my dear."

Rosie reached into the pocket of her skirt, retrieved her notebook, and added a new entry to her list.

It was almost midnight when Max arrived at the Opera House. He did not know what had possessed him to come. These masquerades were always vulgar affairs. It had been years since he engaged in seeking sport among the lower orders. For the sort of women to be found here, he may as well have prowled the streets near Covent Garden.

The deliciously low nature of the entertainment, however, was precisely what drew some of the aristocracy and other high-borns to attend.

Lady Samantha Kirby, a young wanton left to her own devices by her gamester husband, had invited Max to be among her party this evening. She was a brazen creature who had been sending out lures to Max for some time. He had shown no interest, however, finding her rather ordinary and entirely predictable. He had declined the dinner invitation, but agreed to join the group later at the masquerade. He might not have come at all had he not heard she had also invited Rosalind. The possibility of another waltz with her was enough to have him donning a black domino and loo mask.

He had not seen the minx since the Easterbrook

ball, when she had strolled through the terrace doors on Radcliffe's arm. The look on her face had told the entire assembly the young buck had been kissing her. Max had left shortly afterward, not wishing to see what else the girl might do.

He stayed away from Fanny's all week. He had not wanted to face Rosalind for it would mean facing his anger at her behavior. Why should he care if she kissed every man in town? Max had puzzled over it for days. What did it mean that he hated the thought of her kissing anyone else? What did it mean that he could not shake the memory of holding her close on the dance floor? What did it mean that he had not, for once, had to recite contrived flattery from an oft-used and well-memorized litany of seduction, but instead had spoken from the heart words of absolute truth?

This radiant young woman piqued his interest as no other woman had before. He did not like it.

Max had a rule about women. He never allowed a woman the upper hand in a relationship. The merest hint of possessiveness, and he broke it off. He could not bear the thought of a woman running his life, which is precisely what they all meant to do, whether the commitment was marriage or something less formal. He preferred women who wanted no more involvement than he did, who sought nothing more than a few moments of pleasure. Such woman never aroused even a flicker of sentiment.

Max did not understand this absurd obsession with a little country mouse. She was not at all the sort of woman he preferred. It was precisely that difference, of course, that intrigued him. Innocent yet not innocent. Perhaps it was her passionate approach to life, her incessant curiosity and breath-taking, wide-eyed wonder that fascinated him. In that respect, she was as unlike Max as she could be.

Maybe it was true that opposites attract.

He had put on his domino and mask while still in
the hackney, and now made his way toward the stage
where the ball was in progress. Each Opera House
ball had a different theme, utilizing stage settings and
props to suggest various exotic or pastoral settings.
Tonight's set appeared to be a gypsy camp. A painted
backdrop showed a motley caravan, brightly colored
fabric was draped all about, and a covered gypsy
wagon had been placed at the rear of the stage.

The dancers, cavorting with drunken abandon in a
country dance, included harlequins, Turks, nuns,
jesters, shepherds, queens, red Indians, Cavaliers, and
every other sort of character, along with dominos of
every color. Lady Kirby's box was to be on the second tier, and Max made his way upstairs.

Riotous laughter spilled through the partially open
curtain of the box. Max held back the heavy velvet
and glanced inside to find it filled almost to capacity.
He saw a scantily clad huntress—Diana, no doubt—
who was clearly Lady Kirby. She was draped seduc-
tively across a chair, laughing with a tonsured monk
who offered her a glass of wine. Other women included an Indian temple dancer draped in yards of
silk, a shepherdess, and an elaborately garbed Queen
Elizabeth. Two others wore only dominos and masks.
One of them he recognized as Lydia Allardyce, but
he could not have named any of the others. He was,
however, fairly certain none of them was Rosalind.
She must be on stage dancing with one of her swains.

Having surveyed all the women in the box, Max
turned his attention to the gentlemen. Radcliffe was
there, his blond hair giving him away beneath a broad,
plumed cavalier's hat. He was speaking to a page boy
in full glittering green and gold livery. A priest, who
might have been Sir Cedric Bassett, was flirting with
Queen Elizabeth. None of the other domino-clad gen-

tlemen was recognizable, though one might have been Lord Frampton.

None of this company interested him, and so Max drew the curtain closed and made his way toward the stairs. He would see who he could find on the stage. He was halfway down the stairs when he heard footsteps behind him.

"Max!"

He spun around to find the liveried page boy grinning at him. How had he missed her? He ought to have recognized the sensual line of lip beneath the mask. He should have known that mouth anywhere.

"Do you not recognize me, Max?"

"I do now, minx. And how did you recognize me, pray tell? I took such pains with my domino."

"I knew you at once. I could not say precisely what gave you away. Your chin. Your hair. Your shoulders. The way you walk. Any number of things. But I knew it was you. Why are you leaving so soon?"

"I am not leaving. I was on my way to the stage to see if there were any minxes willing to dance with me."

"Oh, famous! I have so been wanting to dance with you again, Max. You are by far the best dancer I know. Let's go!" She grabbed his hand and tugged him along as she dashed down the stairs. "Do you suppose they will play a waltz?"

"I shall see that they do," he said. "I hate to think, though, what will become of my reputation if I am seen to be dancing with a boy."

Rosalind giggled, destroying any attempt to appear as a young man. "Just pull up the hood of your domino, like this. No one will recognize you. Do you like my costume, Max? Fanny helped me with it."

He eyed her up and down, admiring the curve of hip beneath the tight breeches, the long legs and shapely calves. With her short curls artfully tousled

and her slim, tall figure, she did look something like
a boy. But Max was very much aware of the slight
swell of breast beneath the tight-fitting livery jacket
and waistcoat. "You look most fetching, my dear.
Whose page are you meant to be?"

"'I'll have no worse a name than Jove's own page,
and therefore look you call me Ganymede.' Do you
not see my cup?"

She did indeed have a small gold goblet hanging
from her waist as a sort of fob. A modern cup bearer
to the gods. "How stupid of me. Who else would
heavenly Rosalind pretend to be but Ganymede? Shall
I pen verses and hang them about the place?"

Her laughter rang out in the stairwell. "Please do
not. Unless you are a secret Byron?"

"Alas, my verse would be as hackneyed as poor
Orlando's. Let us dance instead, fair Rosalind."

As luck would have it, the orchestra leader informed
Max that the next set was to be a Viennese waltz.

"Is this not an ingenious setting, Max?" she said
as they strolled about the edges of the stage. "I have
yet to see an opera here, and so it is my first visit.
What a fabulously beautiful place this is!"

"I suppose so. I never really noticed." He wasn't
noticing now, either, for he was captivated once again
by her intensity, by the way she hungrily drank in
every detail, eyes and cheeks glowing.

"Oh, how could you not? Only look at the painted
ceiling and the crystal chandeliers. It is almost like a
French chateau. And tier after tier of boxes. How I
would love to see an opera here someday."

"Is that on your list, too?"

She laughed and slapped him playfully on the arm.
"Of course it is. But tonight is an altogether different
sort of treat. All of these spectacular costumes and
laughter and music," she said, and spread her arms

wide. "And the whole stage turned into a gypsy camp. Is it not marvelous?"

Her face flushed so sweetly in her excitement, Max could not resist touching it. He ran a finger against a cheek. It was as soft and warm as he'd expected. "Very clever," he said. She gave a bit of a start at his touch and so he backed off. He ought to leave now before he did something truly stupid. Rosalind was an innocent, not one of his worldly widows. He must keep reminding himself that she was not for him.

Max glanced idly about the stage, avoiding her eyes, when he saw something that might serve as a momentary distraction.

"Do you see the old gypsy woman over there, sitting beneath the wagon?" he asked. "She appears to be reading the tarot cards. Shall we have our fortunes read before the next dance?"

"No!" Her answer was so sharp, he spun around to look down at her. She seemed embarrassed at her brusque response and looked away. "I need no gypsy to tell me my future," she said, her voice so soft he could barely hear her over the noise of the crowd.

How odd. It was the first time he had ever seen the fearless, high-spirited girl refuse to do anything. What was she afraid of?

Chapter 9

"Come along, Max," Rosie said, pulling him by the hand away from the fortune teller. "Let us sit over here and watch the dancing until the waltz begins." She led him to a rustic wooden bench just vacated by a giggling Columbine and a man in Tudor doublet.

"Would you like something to eat, minx? I seem to recall they put on a decent spread here. What do you say?"

"Perhaps just a little something to drink. It is quite warm in here."

He gave her a slow wink. "Wait here. I shall not leave you alone above a moment." He walked away with the languid, rolling grace that would have revealed his identity even in the most concealing costume. Not to mention that strong line of jaw revealed below the mask. She had recognized him in less than an instant.

Rosie experienced a twinge of guilt at having abandoned the others in Lady Kirby's box, especially Lord Radcliffe. The young man had been hanging about her all evening, playing the cavalier with exaggerated chivalry. He had gone so far as to request that he be seated beside her at dinner. Lady Kirby had told her so in confidence while the gentlemen lingered over their port in the dining room. He had already danced with Rosie twice, including a waltz, and clearly intended to maneuver her into a private corner for a kiss. But Rosie had made sure that such an opportunity had not arisen. She liked him well enough, but not enough to warrant another kiss that did not do all those things Fanny had mentioned.

When she had recognized Max, she had run after him with unseemly eagerness. What must he think of her? The simple truth was that Max interested her more than any of her other admirers. Not that Max was an admirer. He probably found her an occasionally amusing departure from his usual women, nothing more. Even so, Rosie could not help but believe that Max above all others could show her some of those pleasures her aunt had mentioned. Who better than the one man of all she'd met who could set her heart to racing with a glance, whose closeness during their waltz had been so intoxicating she had almost swooned, whose whispered flattery was recollected word for honeyed word?

Lord Radcliffe had flattered her, waltzed with her, even kissed her, and yet she felt nothing. She wished it could be otherwise, for no matter how much she wanted Max, she was unlikely to have him. There was no time to waste chasing after a man she could never have.

On the other hand, there was nothing to lose by trying.

Max was as good as his word, returning after barely more than a few minutes, carrying two glasses of wine. "If you hoped for lemonade, you are out of luck, my dear. It is served in the supper room downstairs and would have taken half an hour or more to obtain. Luckily, there are wine tables scattered about."

Rosie took the glass from him. "Wine is perfect, though you must not scold me if I become lightheaded and silly. I've lost count of how many glasses I've had this evening."

"I shall stay on my guard," he said, and seated himself beside her. "Are you enjoying yourself, minx?"

"Oh, yes. Indeed, I have not stopped enjoying myself since I arrived in London."

"And how is the list progressing? What new delights have you enjoyed these last days?" The look in those heavy-lidded eyes could twist the meaning of even the most innocent words.

"Let me see," she said. "I have been to St. Paul's and Westminster Abbey and the Guildhall. I had a delicious lemon ice at Gunter's. I was allowed to drive Mr. Hepworth's cabriolet in the park. I've been kissed. And I saw Mr. Kean at Drury Lane."

Max arched a brow. She expected him to make some remark about being kissed, but instead he said, "Kean, eh? And what did you think of the little man?"

"He was magnificent," Rosie said, breathless at the memory of the extraordinary performance. "He played Macbeth, and I declare I've never seen anything so wonderful. I was positively spellbound."

"I'll bet you were." His voice was full of lazy amusement. Rosie blushed to think what a green rustic she must appear to such a man. "Ah, the reel has ended. Shall we take our places for the waltz, my Ganymede?"

"If you are sure you want to risk your reputation dancing with a boy."

"Anyone who mistakes you for a boy, minx, is a fool whose opinion is not to be considered."

A moment later, Rosie was once again swept up in the pure joy of the dance. The stage was crowded, the other dancers were rowdy and wild and probably drunk. No one noticed or cared that Max held her too close, that his arm was wrapped around her back rather than held decorously at her waist. She closed her eyes and gave herself up to the sheer sensual pleasure of his embrace as he guided her through the waltz.

He did not speak this time. No words of flirtation or flattery, of amusement or seduction. No words at all. His silence allowed Rosie to relish the nearness of him, to appreciate the breadth of his shoulders and the solid muscle beneath her hand, to breathe in the musky male scent of him, to be carried away by the sensual, graceful movements of the dance.

Finally, Rosie opened her eyes to find his gazing down at her with a look that caused her breath to catch in her throat. His gaze moved to her mouth and she unconsciously licked her lips. He is going to kiss me, she thought, and a thrill of anticipation sent her heart to thumping wildly in her breast.

At that moment another couple jostled them, the movement causing Rosie to lose her balance. The moment was lost as well. Max caught her before she stumbled, and the customary glint of amusement had returned to his eyes, replacing the heated expression of a moment before.

Blast! Rosie looked away in frustration, then gasped in sudden horror. Burying her head against Max's shoulder, she said, "Good God! Hide me, Max."

"What the devil?"

"It's my brother," she said in a muffled but agitated whisper. "He mustn't see me!" Blast and double blast. Why did Thomas always have to show up when she was doing something thoroughly improper? Why hadn't he stayed in the Lake District as planned? What an exceedingly tiresome brother he had become.

"Steady, minx. Keep your head down. Which one is he?"

"The tall, dark-haired man in the blue domino dancing with the pink sprite. Is he looking?"

"Not at the moment. The sprite has all his attention. But wait. He does seem to be darting glances in this direction. I don't believe he has quite figured out

who you are. Thinks he recognizes you, but cannot
place you, I suspect."

"Curse it! We must get out of here before he *does*
recognize me."

"Follow my lead, minx."

Max danced them toward the edge of the stage,
then pulled her down the stairs to the stalls. As they
hurried down a side aisle, Rosie glanced over her
shoulder to find Thomas standing center stage, watching them. "Hurry, Max! He's recognized me. Hurry!"

Max swung himself over the side of one of the
lower tier boxes, turned, grabbed Rosie by the waist,
and lifted her up and over into the box. "Beg pardon," he said to the astonished occupants of the box.
Fortunately, they were all thoroughly foxed and thought
it a great lark, laughing merrily as Max tugged Rosie
through the curtain at the back.

Her hand tightly clasped in his, Max hurried along
the crowded corridor and up the first stairway he
found. They passed only one couple on the stairs, and
when they reached the empty landing Rosie pulled
him to a halt.

"Stop!" she cried. She had to catch her breath, but
after a moment, breathlessness was replaced by laughter. She collapsed against Max's chest, laughing too
hard to speak. She could feel his chest shaking with
his own laughter, and it only made her laugh harder.
He wrapped his arms around her and together they
laughed and laughed.

Finally, Rosie pulled away from him, pushed her
mask up onto her head, and wiped her eyes. "Oh,
Max," she said, her voice still quivering with mirth,
"what must those people have thought, to find us
bounding into their box like that?" She dissolved into
giggles once more, thinking of the looks on the faces
of the men and women in the box.

Max removed his own mask, keeping one arm

tightly around her waist. He continued to chuckle softly as he ran a thumb across her wet cheek. He looked younger somehow, laughing and grinning like a boy. "Look what you have reduced me to, minx. Running and leaping about like a madman. If I was recognized, I shall never live it down. And it is all your fault."

Chortling merrily, Rosie considered Max's reputation as a bored sophisticate, loathe to exert himself more than was absolutely necessary. "You are caught out, Max. I knew all that cynical ennui was no more than a fashionable pose."

"Be quiet, minx," he said, and forced her to do so by lowering his mouth to hers.

He kissed her. Thoroughly. He nibbled and tasted slowly, tenderly, as though savoring ripe fruit. After a moment of gentle exploration, he teased open her lips and took her breath away.

His arm tightened around her and he brought the other hand up to run his fingers through her hair, all the while his lips and tongue performed magic with hers. She felt as though her legs would collapse beneath her.

When his lips moved from her mouth to trail kisses down her neck, she thought she had never felt anything so wonderful. It was just like Fanny said it would be. Her toes had quite literally curled up in her slippers.

"What was that about toes?" he murmured against her ear.

Oh, Lord. Had she spoke her thoughts aloud? She turned her mouth toward his and pulled him into another kiss. What better way to keep from uttering nonsense out loud?

The sound of footsteps on the stairs brought a groan from Max, and he ended the kiss. Reluctantly, Rosie thought. The couple hurried past them, staring and sniggering. "Damn," Max said when they had gone.

"Did you know them?" Rosie asked.

"Yes."

"Will they think you were kissing a boy?"

He smiled and gazed down at her with sleepy eyes. "I don't care what they think, my Ganymede. Let me return you to Lady Kirby before you get me into any more trouble."

Max spent only a short time in Lady Kirby's box, accepting a glass of wine but refusing to join the others in a lively *contre danse* right inside the box. He made his excuses and his exit while the most of the party lined up within the confines of the box. Rosalind gave him a wink as she was led down the line on the arm of Frampton.

Lord, what had he done? It was bad enough, the way he had danced with her, though in a masquerade setting, propriety was routinely tossed to the winds. But what the devil had possessed him to kiss her?

Stupid question. She had been perfectly irresistible, that's what had possessed him. Rosalind Lacey had been nearly irresistible since the moment they'd met. Or at least from that second meeting, after she had been transformed from the little brown mouse. Her incredible *joie de vivre* had affected him just as it had every other man. Max had thought himself above the rest, superior to other men in his detachment, his indifference, his dispassionate control.

Yet he was no more immune to her charm than the most callow youth, and he could not have stopped himself from kissing her if he had tried. He had been wanting to kiss her all evening, but each time he came close, he caught himself in time. But her uninhibited, joyous, infectious laughter had been his undoing.

She was irresistible.

She was also an unmarried young woman from the country. Had he just committed himself with that kiss?

Would she now expect him to make an offer? Would Fanny?

Rosalind, however, was not the inexperienced green girl he had thought her to be. The minx playfully admitted to having been kissed by someone else, and demonstrated without question that she knew what she was about. Her words and the look in her eye had been a blatant invitation. She had wanted Max to kiss her, and her response . . . Lord, her response. She had practically melted against him, had kissed him back with exquisite passion, and had even initiated a kiss herself. There was nothing naive or inexperienced about her response. He ought to have known she would approach a kiss with the same enthusiasm she gave to everything else she did.

Egad, but the girl was alive!

Perhaps all she said was true, that she was in town for a lark with no more intention than having a good time. To be sure, she was wide-eyed with wonder, but who wouldn't be at her first experience of the Metropolis? That did not mean she had remained an innocent in Devon. Max recollected that secretive visit from Sir Nigel Leighton.

No, the girl—the woman —was no young innocent. He need not feel obliged to make an offer.

Max experienced a niggling twinge of disappointment. Had he *wanted* to make an offer? Idiot! He wanted nothing of the kind, never had and never would. To be sure, Rosalind Lacey had affected him as no other woman before, but he would not make a fool of himself at this stage in his career. He would, though, take what pleasure he could, and enjoy every moment of it.

As he rode in a hackney on his way back home, Max found himself fingering Freddie Moresby's note tucked out of habit in his waistcoat pocket. He always kept it close as a sort of talisman, to remind him of a way out when boredom overwhelmed him.

But Max had not been bored in weeks. Without conscious thought, the notion of following Freddie's lead had been discarded some time ago. Rosalind's tireless energy, the way she grabbed life by the horns and held on had not only affected him, it had infected him. When was the last time he'd scrambled about the Opera House, jumping into private boxes, stealing kisses in stairwells? When was the last time he'd laughed so hard? When had he last felt so young?

After so many years of raking about town that nothing piqued his interest, Max found himself wanting to absorb some of Rosalind's vitality. He wanted to feel as alive as she did, not bored literally to death. Like Freddie.

If only Freddie had met someone like Rosalind Lacey, he might still be alive.

Rosie awoke the next morning with another pounding headache. Still not as severe as those she'd suffered at home, it nevertheless reminded her of how little time she had left. She curled up on the chaise near the fire and sat quietly for a half hour, sipping the tea Violet had brought.

Ignoring the pain in her head, she contemplated the activities of the evening before. To be perfectly truthful, she contemplated Max's kiss and little else. As enjoyable as the masquerade had been, nothing could compare with those precious moments in his arms. Every detail was recalled to mind: the softness of his lips, the expert way he used them, the taste of wine on his tongue, the caress of his hand against her back, the touch of his fingers in her hair.

Fanny had said the right man would make her feel exactly as she had felt last night with Max. What would her aunt say if she knew Rosie had found the right man, and it was none other than her late lover's son?

Thank heaven she had lived long enough to experience Max's kiss. She would hate to have missed such a moment. And yet, Rosie could not help but think of the other things Fanny had told her, about making love. What were the chances Rosie would have the opportunity to experience that pleasure as well? With Max? Improper and shocking as such thoughts were, she could not deny having them. She knew that making love with Max would be even more wondrous than kissing him, but also know it was a futile dream.

Fanny had said it was best when one was in love. Well, Rosie was as close to being in love as she'd ever been, but the same was not true of Max. He'd told her with pride that he'd never been in love, hinting that it was something to be avoided at all costs. It was hopeless to believe she could change his mind in so short a time.

The headaches came now almost every morning, and Rosie was fairly certain her mother's, though more severe, had never been as frequent.

There was not much time left.

No time to sit around and coddle the wretched headache. She rose slowly from the chaise, gauging the pain to be subsiding, and began to prepare for the day.

Fanny joined her in the morning room some time later, looking stylish as ever in a dress of primrose floret sarsnet flounced with French trimming. She asked about the masquerade and teased Rosie about overindulging. "How you manage to avoid having a thick head every morning I shall never know, what with all the wine and champagne and such. Never rise before noon myself when I've had more than three glasses the night before. But you are looking especially cheerful this morning, my dear, and just the tiniest bit smug."

Rosie grinned, thinking how hopelessly transparent she must be. And here she thought she had been playing the role of Rosalind the Sophisticate so well.

"I am all ears," Fanny said. "Tell me what happened."

"Well, it was a perfectly splendid affair. Gorgeous costumes, a spectacular gypsy camp setting, glorious music. Loads of people were there. It was much more crowded than any of the private balls we've attended. It was fun trying to guess who was who. Oh, and you will be pleased to know my page costume was a grand success."

"I am certain it was. Not every woman can carry off a breeches role, but your slim figure is perfect for it. Saw Mrs. Jordan during her last run at Covent Garden, still playing your namesake in her fifties. Poor thing ought to have given up breeches parts long before—she had grown much too stout to be convincing as a boy. But I am glad your own short run as Ganymede went off well. I did so admire that cunning little fob-cup. An inspired accessory, if I do say so. Anyone interesting at the ball?"

"Scores of vulgar types, most of whom did not recognize me as a woman, thank heaven, for they were most of them foxed and free with their attentions. There was one interesting moment, though, when an unknown gentlemen making all sorts of flirtatious advances discovered I was not a boy. He was exceedingly disappointed."

"Ha! But who else was there?"

"The usual crowd."

"All of your beaux?"

"Most of them."

"And did you receive another kiss? Is that why you look so pleased with yourself?"

Rose gave a self-conscious grin. "If you must know, yes, I was kissed."

"Better this time?"

"Exceedingly so."

"Well done, my girl! Radcliffe again?"

"No."

"Who, then? Oh, don't give me that look as though it were none of my business. Of course it is not. But you must know that I am merely curious and will not rip up at you like some stiff-necked chaperone. Give an old woman a vicarious thrill. Tell me who kissed you."

"Max."

Fanny's brows crept up beneath the lace of her cap and her jaw literally dropped. "Max Davenant? My Max?"

Rosie nodded.

"Well, well." Fanny shook her head and a smile crept across her face and lit her eyes. "Did a proper job of it, did he?"

"My toes curled."

Fanny let out a crack of laughter. "I am sure they did. If anyone knows how to make a woman's toes curl, it is Max. My, my, my."

Fanny came and sat beside Rosie and clasped her hand. "You know that I adore Max," she said, "but you must be careful, darling. He may offer extraordinary pleasure, but he is not a man likely to offer any sort of commitment."

"And I am not looking for one. Only for a bit of enjoyment while I'm in town."

"You are certain of that?"

Rosie heaved a sigh. "Quite certain. Have I not said as much over and over since the day I arrived? An adventure or two, a bit of fun, then I'll be off to Devon and no one will even remember me."

"I would not count on that, my dear." Fanny squeezed Rosie's hand. "As for Max, I wish that you may find pleasure with him, my dear. He is a marvelous man, very much like his father. You are fortunate to have caught his eye. But you must take care. I should feel dreadful if you were to return to my brother in an interesting condition. Edmund would have my head."

"Do not worry, aunt. Such an event will not occur."

"You are so confident you can resist him?"

Rosie smiled. "No. But there would be no awkward consequences. It is quite impossible."

Fanny cocked a brow. "Oh?" She gazed quizzically at Rosie for a moment, then her expression softened. "Oh. Oh, my dear girl. I understand."

Rosie was quite at odds to explain what it was her aunt understood, but was not given the opportunity to inquire. Fanny patted her hand, then walked to the door and summoned a footman. "I am off to Lydia Newbury's. I'd invite you to come along, but I fear you would find a bunch of gossiping old women a dead bore. Besides, I suspect some young swain is scheduled to take you driving again this afternoon, eh?" She reached a hand to her silver hair, insuring the waves were in place. "I shall see you this evening, my dear. The Ingalls's rout, is it not?"

In a flutter of primrose skirts, she was gone.

How extraordinary. If Rosie was not mistaken, her aunt had just pronounced her approval of a love affair with Max. She smiled, thinking how outraged her sisters would be. Ursula would remind them all that she had warned against Rosie staying with Aunt Fanny, had predicted that just such a thing might happen.

Thank God Rosie had ignored them all and followed her instincts.

A moment later, the butler entered to announce that Miss Lacey had a visitor. "A young gentleman," he said and presented a card on a silver tray. With one glance at the card, Rosie's heart sank.

Thomas.

He was bound to have tracked her down sooner or later. There was no avoiding him now. Blast. "Show him in, Quigley."

A moment later he returned with her brother. "Mr. Thomas Lacey," he said, and then made a discreet exit.

Thomas stood in the doorway and gaped. Rosie stood and said, "Hello, Tommy."

"Good God," her brother said at last. "It really *is* you."

"Yes, of course it is. Come in and sit down, Tommy. You have just missed our aunt. Would you like some tea?"

He made no move to enter the room, still standing on the threshold and staring. "That was you last night, then," he said, "at the masquerade?"

"Yes. "

"And at Almack's?"

"Yes."

"And you are the notorious Miss Lacey whose name is on everyone's lips?"

Rosie shrugged. "I suppose so." He looked so incredulous, so stern, she steeled herself for a ripping scold. She was, therefore, quite astonished when instead he gave a bark of laughter, rushed across the room, swept her up in his arms, and twirled her about.

"Rosie, Rosie! You are a marvel. What has happened to you?"

"Put me down," she shrieked merrily, "and I shall tell you."

He brought her back to earth, took both her hands, and held them out to her sides. "My God, you look wonderful. I can hardly believe it is you! Your hair, your clothes . . . everything. You are positively transformed!"

"I know. I had a lot of help from Aunt Fanny. Oh, Tommy, you must get to know her. She is absolutely marvelous."

"But, what the devil are you doing here? Does Father know?"

"Sit down and stop gaping like a schoolboy, and I shall tell you all about it."

Without mentioning her illness, she told him about deciding to come to London and of Aunt Fanny's invitation. She told him of all she had done—or, almost all—and all the places she'd been and the people she'd met.

"I'm having a splendid time, Tommy. I hope you are not going to spoil it for me."

"Spoil it? Why would I do that? I am pleased beyond measure to see you striking out at last. It is horrid how you have been stuck at Wycombe all these years. Besides, you cannot imagine the cachet I have gained by being the brother of the dashing Miss Lacey. But what prompted all this? Are you hanging out for a husband now that the twins are off at Harrow?"

"No," she answered wearily, tired of constantly having to disoblige everyone of that notion. "I am merely enjoying a few months' visit with my aunt."

"Good thing," he said. "That was Davenant I saw you with again last night, was it not? The man ain't the marrying kind, if you take my meaning. Best be careful there, Rosie."

"Not to worry, Tommy. Max is only a good friend. He is a great favorite of Fanny's, you know. I met him on my very first day in town."

"That reminds me." He began to tug at his waistcoat pocket, and pulled out a folded paper. "Take a look at this. Saw it in a print shop window yesterday."

She unfolded the paper to find a colored print boasting the title "The Scarlet Waltz, or Seventh Heaven Sees Red." The distinctive hand of Mr. Rowlandson showed plump, pink-cheeked figures crowded into a ballroom. In the center, a red-garbed buxom female was held in the indecently tight embrace of a dark-haired gentleman with a distinctive jaw who twirled her about the dance floor. In the background, crimson-faced ladies glared open-mouthed at the spectacle. One of them, with an exaggerated pug nose strongly reminiscent of Mrs. Drummond-Burrell, had dropped to the floor in a dead faint, skirts wafting up above her knees to reveal plump legs and loose garters. Several gentlemen stood over her, leering, while another pinch-faced woman wielded a fan over the prone woman's face.

Beneath the picture was written:

> *When Miss L—— danced with Mr. D——*
> *Her style was quite improper.*
> *The ladies whose rules she defied*
> *Could do nothing to stop her.*
> *She let the gent, a rake renowned,*
> *Take liberties quite shocking.*
> *At least one stickler hit the floor*
> *While others stood there gawking.*

"Good heavens," Rosie said. "Is this supposed to be what I think it is?"

"You and Davenant at Almack's."

"Oh, Lord."

Thomas chuckled. "Capital, ain't it? You're famous, Rosie."

She groaned. "Infamous, I should say. The Scarlet Woman of the Scarlet Waltz."

"Want me to buy 'em all up so one of 'em don't get back to Father? Or, God forbid, Ursula? Talk about seeing red." He gave a shudder.

"Thank you, Tommy, but I suspect you would be too late to buy them all. I shall just have to take my chances. I would be obliged, however, if you kept it to yourself when you return to Wycombe."

"Don't worry, I shan't take it with me. Wouldn't matter, though. Even if someone there were to see it, I cannot believe they would recognize quiet, shy Rosie

Lacey as the buxom wench in the picture. And there must be dozens of Miss L's."

"Quite true."

"But Davenant is frequently lampooned, by both Rowlandson and Cruikshank. That phiz could only belong to one Mr. D. Here, why don't you take this one, Rosie, as a souvenir of your London adventure. In your crotchety old age you can pull it out and remember your grand Season cavorting with rakes."

"You keep it, Tommy. I won't be needing it."

Chapter 10

It had been some time since Max had so actively pursued a woman. Frankly, pursuit had seldom been necessary. Women were generally eager and willing to take Max to their beds.

Rosalind Lacey required pursuing. Not so much because she resisted him, but because she was so damned popular. Every blade and blood worth his salt was angling after her. The minx was in such demand, Max was lucky to have a waltz with her now and then. Always a waltz. Max would not waste his time on a quadrille or a country dance. He wanted to put his arms around her.

His best opportunity at seduction came during a visit to Vauxhall Gardens. It was on Rosalind's list of places to go, and she had cajoled her aunt into making up a party. Fanny was not eager to do so, saying that Vauxhall was not the same since the great cascade had been demolished the year before, but she had finally relented.

Max suspected Fanny knew of his interest in her niece, and hoped she would keep the party small enough to allow him ample opportunity to get Rosalind alone. When word got out, however, that a Vauxhall party was in the works, all of Rosalind's beaux began hanging out for an invitation. The minx obliged most of them. To even out the numbers, she invited several ladies as well, so the box was filled to bursting soon after they arrived.

When Max had secured his waltz, he lost no time in leading her away from the dancing and toward the Dark Walk.

"Have you become bored with our waltzes, Max?" she asked as he took her arm and guided her deeper into the gardens. She wore a pale pink dress with a bodice of burgundy velvet, and an imperial cap in matching velvet, ornamented with a silver bandeau and beads. She looked good enough to eat. "I take leave to tell you that I have not," she said. "No one dances as well as you do, you know. I so look forward to our waltzes."

"As do I, minx. But tonight, I look forward to other things."

"Yes, there is so much to be seen here, is there not? The charming orchestra pavilion, the music, the rope dancers, the jugglers, the Turkish alcoves, the transparencies, the Grand Salon, the lights—Oh, Max, the lights! So many lanterns glittering through the trees. It is like a fairyland, is it not? And there are—"

"Come here, minx." He pulled her into a dark, wooded alcove and took her in his arms. "This is what I have looked forward to."

He kissed her hungrily and she responded in kind, molding herself to him like a second skin. He wanted her so badly, he would have taken her then and there, but it was not his style. He would do it properly or not at all. Instead, he kissed her deeply and was just about to caress her more intimately when a loud explosion was followed by flash of light in the sky.

She pulled away and looked up. "Oh, Max! It's the fireworks! Let us go watch them." She took his hand and tugged him along, back to the main walk and toward the supper pavilions where the view was best. Soon, she was lost to him in the excitement of the spec-

tacle, and he cursed himself for not watching the time.
He ought to have known she would not want to miss
the fireworks. He was unable to manage another private moment with her the rest of the evening.

Like a lovesick puppy, Max continued to dog her
movements, making an appearance at every event he
knew she would attend, becoming as much a fixture
as her devoted coterie of swains. His interest was noticed, and his friends began to taunt him.

"Thought you were out of the game," Lord Vaughn
had complained. "No sense competing if you're in."

"Unfair advantage," Hugh Jeffries grumbled.
"Thought I might catch her eye. Don't stand a chance
now. Dammit, Davenant, you might have said something."

He ignored their jibes and continued his pursuit.
And each time he saw her smile, each time he joined
in her laughter, each time he touched her, each time
he held her in his arms during a waltz, each time he
listened to her bright-eyed, exuberant, joyful account
of some new wonder, she stole another little piece of
his heart.

It had been a dozen years and more since it last happened, but he recognized all the signs. He was falling
in love with her.

Max had avoided being a party to Rosalind's afternoon excursions when, guidebook in hand, she explored every corner of the Metropolis. He had,
however, developed a fond anticipation of her ani-
mated, and frank, descriptions of each outing. She
adored the Tower, but hated its menagerie, preferring
Polito's at Exeter Change. She was disappointed in
Bullock's Museum on Picadilly, but had been thrilled
to see Napoleon's carriage on display. The British Museum had been a dead bore, but the Elgin Marbles
sent her into raptures.

Max had, for once, beat out the competition and

obtained the privilege of driving her through the park one afternoon shortly after the Vauxhall party. Beguiled by her rhapsodic recital of the beautiful works to be seen at the latest exhibition of the Society of Painters in Water-Colours in Lower Brook Street, he was unprepared for the clever trap she set and fell straight into it like the greenest gull.

"Have you seen the current exhibition?" she asked.

"No, I haven't had the pleasure."

"You must take the time to do so, Max. You do not know how fortunate you are here in London to be able to see the best and brightest in every field. Do you enjoy painting? Oh, but of course you do. Aunt Fanny told me of your collection of modern works. I find myself most intrigued by Mr. Turner. Are you fond of his work?"

"Very much so. I own two of his paintings."

"Do you? Then you must of course be anxious to see the new ones on view at the Royal Academy exhibition. I had planned to visit Somerset House tomorrow. I should be pleased to have your escort, Max. You may explain to me Mr. Turner's vision and technique."

And so Max found himself ushering Rosalind through the crowded rooms, catalog at the ready, examining new works by Academy artists. Max always made a point of viewing all new Academy exhibitions, but usually by private arrangement and with an eye toward purchase. This time, with Rosalind at his side and the crowd of spectators jostling them about, he found more enjoyment than he would have imagined. It was gratifying and stimulating to share reactions with another. She had a definite eye for color and light, and was brutally frank in the expression of her opinions.

There were new works to be seen by Lawrence ("glossy bravura"), Wilkie ("exquisite sentiment"),

Chantrey ("tender pathos"), Samuel ("a dabbler"), Fuseli ("horrifically sublime"), Martin ("portentous"), Ward ("I detest equine portraits"), and Mulready ("derivative"), as well as a massive work by Turner representing the *Decline of the Carthaginian Empire*. Rosalind read aloud from the catalog that it was a companion piece to *Dido Building Carthage* exhibited two years before.

"I recollect that one," Max said. "I believe this to be more successful in the subtlety of lighting."

"It is glorious, but—"

"The man's work is an outrage," a voice behind them boomed. "It is an offense to the eye and ought not be displayed in public."

Rosalind's lips pursed in anger and she spun around to face the harsh critic. "I beg your pardon, sir, but— Uncle Talmadge!"

Lord Talmadge, a stout, florid gentleman nearly bald as an egg, puffed out his chest and glared at Rosalind over the edge of gold spectacles perched precariously on a bulbous nose. "And who might you be, madam?"

"Do you not recognize your own niece? I am Rosalind Lacey."

He reared back and squinted through the spectacles. "Lacey? One of that brood, eh? How should I be expected to recognize one of—how many? Dozens?"

"There are six of us, as you well know. Or would, if you took the least interest in your sister's family."

"Impertinent hussy!" The man's face turned a deep red and he looked near to apoplexy. "As though I cared a fig for any brats sired by that fool Louisa married. Never approved of the man or his loathsome family. That sister of his racketing about town, setting herself up as some sort of courtesan to the Prince of Wales. Spawn of the devil, she and all her kin. Want nothing to do with any of you. Be off now, girl."

"How dare you speak like that of my family, you hateful old man." Her voice had grown loud and Max was dismayed to see a crowd begin to gather. "Your own sister's family! Allow me to tell you to your head that we want none of you, either, my lord. Is this gentleman a friend of yours?" she asked, nodding to the gaunt, elderly man standing next to Lord Talmadge. "Did you know, sir, that his fine lordship refused even to acknowledge any of his own sister's children? That he never answered his sister's plea for help the year my father's crops failed and we had barely more than two shillings to rub together? That the only time he was persuaded to darken the doors of our home was when he came to demand return of a family bible my mother cherished? That he never bothered to attend her funeral, or even to acknowledge her death? Christian charity, indeed."

"Impudent girl! I knew no good would come of marriage with a Lacey. Come along, Abernathy. I've had enough of this sharp-tongued baggage, as well as these monstrous splatters of paint. Let us leave this godless den of wickedness!"

The gaunt man was pulled roughly along by Lord Talmadge, but continued to stare over his shoulder in open-mouthed astonishment until he had disappeared into the crowd. The confrontation had drawn a large group of bystanders who began to whisper and snigger as they stared at Rosalind.

Max had kept hold of Rosalind's arm the whole time, and now guided her away from the crowd. "Perhaps we should leave," he said. "You cannot enjoy the pictures now. Come along, minx."

She walked stiffly at his side, head held high on her long, elegant neck, chin lifted at a defiant angle. She looked as imperious and proud as any duchess and drew many an appreciative glance as they made their way to the exit.

Max settled her in his carriage and gave the driver instructions before joining her. He took her chin in his hand and turned her face toward him. Her eyes were bright with unshed tears, and yet a smiled tugged at the corners of her mouth. "I have always wanted to do that," she said, "to tell him exactly what I thought of him."

"You made an excellent job of it, minx. He deserved every blow you landed."

"Yes, he did. It is just so frustrating!" She pounded the bench with a fist. "There was never any need for him to be estranged from Mama, though God knows she was probably better off without him. But she was his sister! And the irony of it is that Papa felt the same way about his own family. He has always been ashamed of Fanny and her notoriety. My uncle ought to have approved of him. Papa is a quiet, reserved country gentleman who finds more pleasure in his books than in his family. Though not as sanctimonious as Uncle Talmadge, he is very much steeped in propriety."

Max guessed that Rosalind's gregarious, lively personality was a reaction against such a parent. "How the devil did you get him to agree to let you stay with Fanny?"

"I am well above the age where I need his consent," she said, "but even so, he was quite accommodating. He was not thrilled, to be sure. He would rather I had gone with starchy old Lady Hartwell, who chaperoned both my sisters during their Seasons. But Fanny intrigued me. When I boldly wrote to ask if I might visit her, she obliged by writing Papa and inviting me."

"Capital woman, Fanny."

"She is. And it saddens me that so many of my family think otherwise. I am *so* glad I have got to know her. Uncle Talmadge can be damned. Aunt Fanny is worth a hundred of him."

"And so are you, minx." Max kissed her gently on the mouth, without passion, and knew in that moment that he was completely, foolishly, deliriously in love with her.

She smiled up at him, then rested her head on his shoulder. "Do you have any loose screws in your family, Max?"

"Had a great uncle who lost his wits and had to be locked up in an attic for years."

"Oh!"

"But I am sorry to report that most of my relations are frightfully upstanding. My eldest brother, Ethan—he's the current Earl of Blythe—minds the family estates with great care. Married well, and his wife has dutifully presented him with three sons and a daughter. Old Ethan is a pillar of the community. Then there's my sister Adelaide, Lady Gresham. Married a marquess with buckets of money, and spends it all on various charitable causes. Always doing good works, is Adelaide. Funding some school or hospital. And finally we have my younger brother, Trevor, Colonel Davenant of the 16th Light Dragoons. Made a name for himself with Wellington, listed in any number of dispatches. A hero at Waterloo. Now on Castlereagh's staff."

"What a remarkable family you have," Rosalind said. "You must be quite proud."

"Quite." The achievements of his siblings were indeed a source of pride for Max, but also a burden. He had never been able to match their productive lives, and ceased trying at an early age. Instead, he decided to dedicate his life to pleasure, and could boast that he had succeeded, reaching the top of his "profession."

"Speaking of siblings," he said, "whatever became of that brother of yours who stalked us at the Opera House?"

Rosalind lifted her head from his shoulder and smiled. "He came around to Fanny's the next day. Believe it or not, he didn't rip up at me at all. Thought it was grand lark."

"Not everyone in your family, then, is a stuffed shirt."

"No, but my sister Ursula makes up for the rest. You will never meet anyone higher in the instep than Ursula."

"I shall do my best to avoid her."

"Where are we going, Max?"

"To Gunter's. I thought you might need a lemon ice to cool you down after that fiery outburst."

A smile broke across her face, bright and fresh as a sunrise. "Excellent!"

"You told him he was a hateful old man?"

Rosie giggled at her brother's look of astonishment. "I did, and it felt wonderful. Hurry up with my cravat, Tommy. I am all agog to be off."

"Can't believe how you've changed, Rosie. Telling off old Talmadge. Curricle racing."

"I won!"

"Yes, I know. The whole world knows. And now this. Don't know how you managed to talk me into this caper."

"You said I passed easily as a boy at the masquerade."

"A costume ball is one thing. People think nothing of a female in breeches. But this ain't a masquerade, Rosie. If we're caught, I'll be a laughingstock."

"No, you won't. You may simply say that your notorious sister is touched in the upper works and you wash your hands of her. Besides, why should men have all the fun? You have mills and clubs and cock fights—though I don't believe I should enjoy watching chickens tear each other to pieces—and gaming hells and who knows what all. I have promised myself I would sample all that London has to offer, even if I have to disguise myself as a man to do it. How do I look?"

Thomas eyed her up and down, then walked around her in a slow circle. She was wearing a pair of his own breeches that fit snuggly at the waist and hips but were a shade too long, along with a shirt, waistcoat, and jacket borrowed from a friend closer to her size. Thomas admitted he'd been honest enough to tell the young man that his sister needed them, but had implied it was for a masquerade, not a disguise.

"You'll do," he said at last. "But let's keep to the shadows. And don't forget our cover."

"I am Ross Lacey, your sixteen-year-old cousin fresh from the country." Yet another role to play.

"Just so. Lord, I hope you ain't discovered, my girl. Father will skin me alive if he finds out."

She was not, however, discovered.

Their first stop was a sparring match at the Fives Court. It had been a battle to get Thomas to agree to bring her, apparently thinking her delicate sensibilities would be affronted by the sight of men naked to the waist, sweating and grunting and pummeling one another. When she announced her intention to go without him, he relented.

Sparring was not as good as a real mill with a purse, Thomas told her, but often tolerably good sport. The Westminster Fives Court was a cavernous building packed shoulder to shoulder with men of all ranks of society. Near the center was a raised square platform, like a stage, with ropes stretched all around it. The din was deafening as two combatants were cheered on by the mob.

Rosie was at first glance slightly sickened by the sight of blood streaming down the face of one of the men, but the bout soon ended with both men seeming to be in fit shape. A second bout began soon after.

The two men, bare-chested and well-muscled, approached the center of the ring and shook hands. Facing each other, they stood one foot forward, knees bent, gloved fists held at chin level, then began to parry blows. Thomas tried to explain the rules and the science of the ring, but the noise was too loud for Rosie to hear all he said.

She was soon, however, caught up in the excitement, cheering on her brother's favorite, wincing now and then at a particularly fierce blow, and sending up a whoop when the favorite bested his opponent.

Some of Thomas's friends invited him to join them at the Daffy Club, and Rosie cajoled him into taking her along. She was pleased to note that none of the young men suspected her true identity. As a young boy, she was ignored for the most part, barely tolerated as an encumbrance by Thomas's friends.

The Castle Tavern was a gathering place for the Fancy, connoisseurs of pugilism. The long room in the back, known as the Daffy Club, was fitted up with several tables set together to form one long table. The walls were lined with framed sporting prints and illuminated by gas lights. The table was crowded with men, primarily Dandies and Corinthians, though Thomas pointed out a few famous prize-fighters, old standers including the great Belcher himself, who received the homage of their admirers.

Rosie was unable to follow most of the conversations going on around her. They spoke of doublers, digs, and choppers, of claret jugs, nobs, and mufflers, of corner coves and Broughtonians. She had no idea what they were talking about.

Before long, a tankard was placed in front of her. Taking an experimental sip, Rosie discovered it to be gin and was sent into a fit of coughing. She felt a tug on her arm and found Thomas, cocking his head toward the door.

"Come along, *cousin*. You're too young for gin. My uncle will have my head if I get you tanked up on Hollands."

Rosie had no objection to leaving. She found nothing particularly entertaining about a bunch of loud, disorderly gentlemen, foxed to their eyeballs, yammering on about this bout or that race. No wonder women never made a push for entry into these male bastions. They were deadly dull.

"Dammit, Rosie, I'm taking you home. The Fives Court was enough. I ain't taking you anyplace else."

"No, Tommy! Please. We haven't been to a gaming hell yet." At least she could depend upon entertainment at a hell. Rosie was very good at cards.

"Oh, Lord." Thomas grabbed his head and groaned. "I swear, you are going to owe me for this. Where the devil am I supposed to take you? Can't get you into Whites. We'll have to go to Jermyn Street. Know of a little establishment there that ain't too rough."

They took a hackney to the club, a nondescript building in an alley off Jermyn Street. Inside, it was crowded, though much quieter than the Daffy Club. The only sounds seemed to be the slapping of cards on a table, the rattle of dice in a cup, the clinking of glasses, and the occasional murmur of the players. Games of faro and hazard and macao were taking place at tables scattered about the room. Men stood behind the chairs, watching the play and drinking wine or coffee. Waiters quietly meandered about the room, delivering drinks on silver trays. It all seemed very sedate and very serious.

"Whatever you do," Thomas whispered, "don't sit down at a table. You'll be marked for a pigeon and plucked before you can blink an eye. It's deep play,

Rosie. Don't even think of getting into a game. Just watch. Nothing more."

Thomas found a couple of friends and stood with them at a faro table running at high stakes. Rosie wandered about from table to table, finally making her way to one that had gathered the largest group of spectators. It was a hazard table. The player was apparently on a winning streak, causing soft gasps from the spectators with every throw of the dice.

Rosie nudged her way closer, and was startled to find the player was Max. Her gasp of surprise matched those of the spectators as he won again, and more chits were added to his side of the table.

"Good Lord, it's Davenant." Her brother's voice came as a mere whisper in her ear. "He is accounted one of the best hazard players in town."

"How does he win?" she whispered. "I don't understand the game."

Thomas quietly gave her the bare details of hazard. She watched in quiet awe as Max won time after time, never once throwing out. His concentration was fierce, eyes sharp beneath the sleepy lids. Though it was a game of chance, Thomas explained that a really good player could master the odds, and Max seemed to have done so.

When Max, who played standing, had amassed a considerable stack of winnings, he stepped back and called for a glass of wine. His glance swept over the group of spectators, passed over Rosie, then jerked back to stare at her. He arched a brow. Rosie, trying to look masculine, nodded an acknowledgment. Max took the glass of wine offered by a waiter and downed it in two swallows. He signaled that his winnings should be collected and cashed in, then made his way toward Rosie and Thomas.

"Mr. Thomas Lacey, I believe," he said, addressing her brother.

Thomas fidgeted awkwardly, and said, "Yes, I am Lacey."

Turning toward Rosie, Max said, "And this must be . . ."

"Er . . . this is my cousin, Ross Lacey."

"Ross, is it? How delightful to make your acquaintance, young man."

Rosie was hard pressed not to dissolve into giggles. Max seemed to sense her dilemma and steered her and Thomas toward an unoccupied corner of the room.

"I don't suppose this is your idea, Lacey?" he said in a low whisper.

"Lord, no!"

"I thought not. Rosalind—that is, Ross—you are an incorrigible minx. Has she always been so uncontrollable, Lacey?"

"Actually, no. Don't know what's got into her."

"Dare I ask what brings you here, minx?"

"I wanted to see a gaming hell," Rosie said. "You know how I love cards. I thought it would be fun to see how men play when women aren't around."

"And what have you discovered?"

"That men have lots more money with which to gamble. Or at least control of more money. I suspect some of these gentlemen are losing their wives' dowries and their children's futures."

"That may be so. However, I was not losing, as you may have noticed. Nor was I beggaring some poor sap. I play against the bank."

"I wish I knew how you do it, Davenant," Thomas said. "The dice never seem to fail you."

"Oh, but they do," Max said, "from time to time. Tonight, though, they have been good to me."

"Max," Rosie said, "you will never believe all I have done this evening."

"Indeed?"

"Yes, it has been great fun! First we—"

"Lacey! Lacey!" Thomas's friend, who'd been introduced earlier that evening as Jack Loring, came bounding up to him, then practically screeched to a halt when he saw Max. "Oh, I say. Davenant, isn't it? Didn't know you were a friend of Lacey's. Name's Loring. Honored to meet such a prime gamester. Heard you had quite a streak tonight. Bit of luck, what?"

Several more minutes of fawning appreciation followed. The young man was obviously in awe of Max, not only for his skill at the tables, but for his particular mode of dress. Rosie had learned early on that Max was not only exceedingly attractive to women, but was very much admired by other gentlemen as well. He was always beautifully dressed, precise to a pin. When asked by Mr. Loring for advice on achieving the subtle but artistic folds of his neckcloth, Max replied that it was purely accidental. He'd caught Rosie's eye, and she rolled her gaze heavenward, for she knew he was bamming the young man. He'd probably spent hours perfecting his neckcloth.

It was some time before Mr. Loring recollected his errand. "I say, Lacey. Came to tell you. That little Covent Garden dancer you've been dangling after has been giving Challinor the fish eye all evening. Met him in the green room after the first act. Told me she was his for the taking, and he meant to take her tonight. Thought you should know. Might want to beat him to the punch."

Thomas blushed scarlet and dragged his friend out of earshot. Max chuckled. "Poor Thomas. No man wants his sister to know about such things. But then, you aren't like most sisters, are you?"

After a hushed conversation with his friend, Thomas returned. "I'm taking you home, Rosie. Said you'd owe me for tonight. Well, I'm calling in my vowels right now. You've had your fun. Now, let's go."

"Hold on, Lacey," Max said. "You'll never reach Covent Garden in time if you have to drive all the way back to Berkley Square. Go on with Loring. I'll see your young *cousin* safely home."

Thomas looked back and forth between them, apparently weighing his brotherly obligations.

"Don't worry, Tommy. Max and I are old friends. You can trust him to take me back to Fanny's."

He cocked a skeptical brow, but was distracted by Mr. Loring's urgent pleas to hurry. "All right," he said at last, and offered a hand to Max. "Thanks, Davenent. See that she gets home safely." He was out the door a moment later.

Chapter 11

"Well, my Ganymede," Max said, "let us be off." She looked every bit as appealing as she had at the masquerade and he wanted to get her out of here before those long, shapely legs led him to make a public fool of himself.

"Oh, Max, can we not stay for a while longer? I would love to learn to play hazard, though I confess I haven't much money."

"I could not let you lose what little you have in such a place, my dear. It's a fast game, and the bank will have your poor blunt before it's out of your pocket."

"Can you not show me how it is played without the bank? Could I not simply play against you, with no stakes?"

She was tenacious as a terrier. "You are a stubborn minx, aren't you? Let me see if a private room is available."

Within a few moments, Max was leading her into a small room in the back, one of many used for private games with private stakes. A waiter carried in a steaming silver bowl and two goblets, then retired, pulling a heavy velvet drapery across the door.

The other patrons would no doubt think he'd found himself a plump young pigeon to pluck in private. Or worse. But if she insisted on staying, her disguise might be discovered, so it was best to keep her away from prying eyes. Of course, having her all to himself was no small advantage.

"We shall make a night of it, minx. Imaginary stakes and rum punch. It's a bit chilly for May. This brew should warm our bones."

"Rum punch? How marvelous! I've never tried it."

He poured her a glass and she sipped cautiously. A flicker of surprise crossed her face, then she took a long swallow. She closed her eyes and he could almost feel her savoring the sweetness of rum and the tang of lemon juice as it slid down her throat. Head thrown back, lips slightly parted in a blissful smile, she looked positively beatific. If he hadn't been afraid of someone interrupting them, he'd have kissed her then and there.

"You look like you've died and gone to heaven," he said.

She opened her eyes and smiled. "Not yet," she said. "Oh, Max, it is delicious. This is one thing I begrudge men keeping to themselves. Shall I tell you about my evening?"

And she did. He joined in her excitement over the Fives Court match, and laughed at her description of the unintelligible language and gin-induced choking at the Daffy. "Are these breeches roles going to become a habit with you, minx?"

"I confess, it is more comfortable to be unencumbered by skirts. But I doubt I shall take up the style permanently."

"After tonight, you must surely have completed everything on your list. Can there be anything left you have not yet done?"

She gave him a look worthy of the most skilled temptress. "I have not played hazard," she said.

And so Max set about explaining the rules, which were simple enough, and demonstrating how to keep track of the odds. They laughed and played and drank

for more than an hour. When he realized she was becoming tipsy from the punch, he decided it was time
to leave.

"Remember, minx, you are young Mr. Ross Lacey.
Keep steady and keep quiet. And for God's sake, don't
giggle."

She did giggle, but recovered quickly, standing
straight and tall when he pulled back the velvet curtain.

He collected his winnings, paid his shot, and bun-
dled Rosalind out the door. She remained admirably
composed and steady on her feet while he hailed a
hackney, but collapsed into a limp heap once inside.
She fell against him, so warm and soft he wanted to
devour her. He lifted her onto his lap and she snuggled up to him like a kitten. She lifted her face and
said, "Kiss me, Max. Make my toes curl."

"With pleasure, madam."

The punch had affected them both, and their kiss
was long and slow and succulent. They kissed until
the hackney came to a stop. "You are disastrous to
my reputation, minx. I am forever being seen kissing
a young boy."

"Then let us go somewhere more private."

There was no mistaking her invitation. It was what
he wanted, what he had wanted for weeks, and now
it was what she wanted, too. But was it only the punch
talking?

"Are you sure, minx?"

She smiled at him with the same rapture held seen
when she first tried the rum punch. "Quite sure."

"I would not have you regretting it tomorrow."

"I will only regret it if you do not make love to
me, Max."

Oh, God. "Rosalind." He kissed her again, forgetting himself until the driver slid back the opening and
asked if his bloody lordship was going to be all night.

Max lifted Rosalind out and paid the driver, who hurried off muttering something about Queer Street and the Quality.

"Where are we?" Rosalind asked.

"At my house. We're on Mount Street, just a few steps from Berkley Square. It's not too late to change your mind, Rosalind. I am happy to walk you home. Perhaps we have both had too much punch and a walk in the cool night air will do us good."

She placed a hand on his chest and fingered his lapel. "I thought you were a notorious rake, Max, but here you are trying like mad to talk me out of making love with you. Why?"

He lifted her hand and brought it to his lips. "Because you are not just any woman, Rosalind. You are not like all the rest, who are easy enough to toss between the sheets and then forget. If we make love, I am afraid it will be quite unforgettable."

"So am I, Max. I will be so disappointed if you do not take me inside and make it so."

"There is nothing I would rather do, minx. Come along, then." He took her hand and led her up the steps, using his key to unlock the door. Once inside, he swept her up into his arms and carried her up the stairs.

Rosie lay curled up on her side watching Max sleep. Fanny had been right once again. It had been the most glorious, most wonderful, most extraordinary experience of her life.

They had undressed each other frantically, flinging clothes all about the room. But then Max had taken charge and made slow, delicious, exquisite love to her. Simply being naked with him had been the most incredible thrill. He was beautifully made, with broad chest and slim waist, and she explored every inch of him while he made magic with his hands and mouth in exploration of her own body. He had driven her to the edge of frenzy before he had finally entered her.

There had been only a brief moment of pain for Rosie, and a brief moment of surprise for Max. He had looked down at her and smiled so tenderly it made her feel like weeping. "I wasn't sure," he said. "But I'm glad. I love you, Rosalind, and I don't want to share you with any man. Have I hurt you?"

"No," she had said. "And please don't stop, Max. Just love me."

And he did, quite thoroughly, whispering words of love over and over, which she answered in kind, until she had reached an almost unbearable pinnacle of pleasure and shuddered her release beneath him.

She could die now. The disease could take her right this minute and she would die happy. She had achieved the perfect memory, just as Fanny had said. She had made love with a man she adored, and who loved her in return.

Or did he? He had told her that he sometimes fell in love in the heat of passion, but that the feeling always passed.

It did not matter. All she had hoped for was a single moment of love, however fleeting. It need not be a lasting passion. In fact, it was better if it was no more than momentary for she could not promise anything longer. She had achieved her moment of love, and it had been utterly splendid. She had fulfilled all her dreams, and more, for she could never have dreamed anything could be so utterly wonderful.

Rosie smiled as she watched him sleep. There was something to be said about making love with a rake. All that practice had made him perfect. She could not have asked for a more masterful lover.

But perhaps Max would feel awkward in the morning, knowing he had spoken words of love and knowing he hadn't meant them. Rosie had no wish to make it difficult for him. It would be best if she slipped quietly away before he awoke, thus avoiding a potentially uncomfortable situation. And though she had more or less given her blessing to such an occasion, Fanny might be worried if Rosie did not come home before morning.

She inched toward the edge of the bed, taking care not to jostle Max and wake him. Locating her clothes was difficult, especially in the dark. They were strewn in every corner of the room, entwined with Max's clothes. She managed to find them all and got dressed quickly, leaving her neckcloth loose and untied.

As she glanced in Max's shaving mirror, illuminated by no more than a sliver of moonlight through a gap in the shutters, she saw something propped up against the back of the washstand. Leaning closer, she recognized it as the print of The Scarlet Waltz, showing her and Max dancing together. Thomas had said Max was a frequent target of the caricaturists, but she could see no other prints in the room. It pleased her that he kept it. She wished now that she had taken the one Thomas had offered.

Rosie tip-toed down the stairs and made her way out the front door without disturbing the household. It was not quite dawn, too early for the servants to be about. She walked up Mount Street to where it joined Davies Street, then turned left to enter Berkley Square. She had her own key, since she often kept such late hours, and let herself into Fanny's house.

When she reached her room, exhaustion vied with exhilaration to overwhelm her. She could not have slept if she tried. Images of Max and all he'd done to her swam drunkenly in her head. Her body still ached, pleasantly so, where he had worked inside her. His musky scent still clung to her skin. How could anyone sleep after such a momentous experience?

But fatigue took its toll as well. It had been a long

day. She had been shopping with Lady Kirby, paid calls with Fanny, and driven in the park with Mr. Hepworth. She had then gone to her brother's rooms and begun her transformation into Ross Lacey. She had hardly spent more than five minutes in Berkley Square.

On such busy days, any letters, invitations, or calling cards for Rosie were left on her dressing table. Three letters awaited her now. She undressed and washed her face before taking the letters with her to bed, where she propped herself on a mound of pillows, ready to read.

The first letter was from Jeremy Aldrich, and included a florid ode to Miss Lacey`s eyes. She shuddered and tossed it aside. The second was from her sister Pamela, full of news from home and a hint that she might be increasing. She wrote of the vicar's new wife and how her mother was coming to live at the vicarage. She wrote of the recent betrothal of Sally Griggs and Matthew Penwarren, and of how little Robbie Bascom had fallen out of a tree and broken his arm. She also related an odd bit of news about the new earthenware manufactury in the district being temporarily closed down. Apparently, residual cobalt and other minerals had been dumped into Kennott Rill—an Otter tributary that fed many local pools and ponds—causing sickness among people who drank from those waters. The district council had closed the manufactury down until the owners developed another method of waste disposal. Pamela said it was big news in the district—it must be to warrant an entire paragraph in her sister's cramped script—and that several of Papa's tenants had been taken ill.

The last letter was from Sir Nigel Leighton, and filled several pages. Rosie shuddered with a twinge of anxiety and irritation. No matter how wondrous the evening, there was always her blasted illness to consider. What, though, could the physician have to say to her that required so many sheets? She took a deep breath and read.

He began with a scold, chastising her for never being at home and forcing him to write instead. After several more lines criticizing her late nights and busy days, he got to the point.

"I have received a letter from Dr. Urquhart," he wrote.

It confirmed my suspicions regarding your mother's illness. He says that Lady Lacey suffered a fall from her horse in 1805, during which she struck her head. The injury, though externally minor, caused damage to her brain resulting in a form of epilepsy, which you may know as the falling sickness. The social stigma attached to the condition and its attendant seizures compelled her to keep it secret. Besides Dr. Urquhart, only your father and your mother's nurse knew of it. I would not now break the confidence promised your mother were it not for your own present concerns.

Your mother's headaches and dizziness and especially the coldness in extremities generally preceded a seizure. Apparently, she was successful in sensing when one was about to overtake her, and retired out of view of the rest of the family before it took hold. It is a remarkable testament to her tenacious will and prodigious efforts at controlling the condition that none of you ever witnessed a seizure.

It was during a particularly violent seizure that Lady Lacey struck her head again, this time on the sharp corner of some piece of furniture. Unfortunately, this blow was fatal.

So I can tell you that while your mother's death was indirectly caused by her epilepsy, the condition alone did not kill her. It is not generally a fatal condition. And your mother's form of epilepsy, caused by a blow to the head, is not in any way hereditary.

The conclusion is, Miss Lacey, that you are not suffering from epilepsy.

As to the cause of your headaches, Dr. Urquhart reports that a local china works factory has lately been discovered to be disposing of mineral wastes, particularly cobalt and manganese, into a stream that feeds many local ponds and pools, including one on your father's estate. He has seen many patients suffering from cobalt poisoning as a result, a condition with symptoms that can include headache, dizziness, blurred vision, and coldness in the extremities. I suspect, Miss Lacey, that your own symptoms are those of cobalt poisoning, a result of some sort of repeated contact with the tainted water, especially when we consider the fact that the symptoms ceased when you came to London.

You may rest assured that you are not going to die from your symptoms. Cobalt poisoning is not fatal. I am persuaded that any headache etc, you have suffered since coming to London is a direct result of dissipation. Overindulgence in drink can—

Rosie stopped reading and dropped the pages onto her lap. She sat for several moments, frozen with astonishment.

Could it be true? She was not going to die?

She *had* drunk from Wycombe Pond, which was not only fed by Kennott Rill but also by a natural spring. The fresh mineral water was a guilty pleasure she indulged often as she rode about the estate, so often that any poisoning of the water would surely have affected her. And all because of the factory that produced those lovely blue and white transferware dishes she so admired.

It was incredible news. It was miraculous. It was sensational. She was not going to die! She began bouncing on the bed in her excitement. Dear God, she was not going to die! She was not! Tears of joy clouded her vision as she bounced up and down like a schoolgirl. She was not going to die.

And then realization slammed into her gut like a giant fist and twisted her stomach into knots.

Oh God. Oh no, no, no. This was terrible news. Dreadful. Horrible. She was not going to die.

She had spent the last two months living literally as though there was no tomorrow, behaving scandalously, doing outrageous things, shaming her family—all because she was going to die so none of it mattered. And now she wasn't going to die?

Dear God in heaven, she had just lost her virginity, given it away, ruined herself with a notorious rake, and now she wasn't going to die?

She let out a wail of despair. "No, no, no!" she moaned, and pounded the mattress with her fists. It wasn't fair. It just wasn't fair! She was supposed to die. She would never have done any of those things if she'd known she wasn't going to die. Wearing immodest, revealing dresses; racing curricles through the park; waltzing without permission; attending Opera House masquerades; publicly castigating her uncle; dressing as a boy to attend sparring matches, gin mills, and gaming hells; giving up her virginity to Max—she would have done none of it if she had known she was not going to die.

Instead, she would live to face the consequences.

Panic grabbed her by the throat. The consequences. She thought of what had just occurred between her and Max and began to feel sick with dread. What if . . .

It was too late. The damage was done. She now had to face the consequences of her actions, to pay the price for impropriety, for self-indulgence, for wanton recklessness. How was she to do it? She was no longer the dashing Miss Lacey up to every rig and row. That mask had been removed forever upon reading Sir Nigel's letter. She was just plain Rosie again, the brown country mouse.

How on earth was Rosie of Wycombe Hall going to live with the repercussions of all the mischief, and perhaps worse, created by Rosalind of Berkley Square? How was she to face her father, knowing she had brought shame and scandal to his name by casually tossing her own reputation to the winds? And Ursula. What would her sister do if and when she discovered all that Rosalind had done? Would they ostracize her? Send her off to live in some remote village in the north with a paid companion? Thomas knew what she'd been up to, of course, and would likely help to conceal as many of her crimes as possible. He would not think the worse of her for what she'd done. But he did not know she'd ruined herself with Max.

Fanny would surely be disappointed to discover all her efforts had been for naught, that the country mouse could not be so easily transformed, that she was her father's daughter after all. Fanny had several times said that Rosie reminded her of herself in younger days. She wanted Rosie to be like her, but she was not. Without that false death sentence, Rosie would never have been so brave, so capricious, so eager to try anything, to defy convention, to flaunt propriety. It had all been a sham.

And what of Max? That was the cruelest question of them all. What of Max? She had fallen head over heels in love with him; but he, assuming he spoke the truth, had fallen in love with someone else. He loved the vibrant, high-spirited, devil-may-care Rosalind. His minx. A phantom who did not exist. A role. A pretense. A lie.

How was she ever to face him again, especially after what they'd just shared. How was she to tell him that the woman he'd loved tonight so sweetly, so passionately, was a fraud? That the woman who promised no regrets was now drowning in them?

Did she regret it? If her ruin became public, she would regret it sincerely. If she became pregnant, she would regret it intensely, for the child's sake. She would regret the label of bastard for any child.

But could she regret the passion, the tenderness, the exquisite pleasure, the words of love? Never. She still had that one perfect memory to last a lifetime.

She would forever, though, regret the way she had deceived Max into believing she was someone else. Rosie thought she'd rather face the wrath of her father than the scorn and disappointment of Max. His contempt would break her heart. She could never see Max again. It would be too painful to explain, to admit the lie.

The best course of action would be to return home at once, confess her shame to Papa, and resume, as best she could, the quiet life of plain, shy, prim Rosie. She must leave Rosalind behind forever. And she must also leave behind Max.

Now she really, really wanted to die.

Chapter 12

Damn! She was gone.

Max must have slept like the dead, which he often did after good sex, since he had not heard a sound. He rose, stretched, and walked to the window. Good Lord, the sun was full up. No wonder Rosalind had crept away. She would have needed to return to Fanny's before light, before anyone was likely to see her. If she had waited for Max to waken, her reputation would be in tatters.

He would, though, have liked to wake and find her soft and warm and naked in his arms. Then he would have made slow, lazy, morning love to her, a pleasure he seldom had the opportunity to indulge. In fact, that is precisely how he would like to spend every morning for the rest of his life.

It was nothing short of extraordinary how that woman had turned his world upside down. A few short months ago, he had grown so weary of the repetitive routine of his life that he had contemplated suicide. Freddie Moresby had been his role model, his shining beacon of enlightenment, because he had found the ultimate solution to boredom: death. Max had been moving inexorably toward that same end. Until he met Rosalind Lacey.

Max folded back the shutters and stood full in the window in all his naked glory, letting the morning sun pour over him. He didn't care who saw him. In fact, he wanted everyone to see him. He wanted to raise the sash, thrust his head out the window, and shout his new happiness to every passerby. He felt like he might explode with ... what? Joy? Max had never felt like this in all his life. It was unnerving. He did not know what to do with all this energy.

It was all because of Rosalind.

She had shown him how to live, how to make the most of every moment. Max no longer contemplated death. He wanted to live. More particularly, he wanted to live with Rosalind.

And that was the most remarkable thing of all. He had been with countless women during his thirty-six years—beautiful women, exotic women, seductive women—and never once had he been tempted to spend more than a night or two now and then with any one of them. Certainly not a lifetime. The very idea would have caused him to break out in a cold sweat.

After one night with Rosalind, however, he found himself entertaining the incredible notion of spending the rest of his life with one woman. Imagine that. The same woman every night. Who could ever have imagined that Max Davenant—philanderer, lothario, rake *extraordinaire*—would even consider such a thing? He flung his arms wide and laughed. What the devil had she done to him?

He rang for his valet and began the long ritual of making himself presentable. He drove poor Hughes to distraction by dawdling, but he kept losing himself in memories of last night. He saw her beautiful, white, slender body, not remotely voluptuous but perfectly proportioned. He felt those soft, ripe breasts crushed against his chest. He saw her long, slim legs wrapped tightly around him. Lord, but she had been a sensual, passionate creature. No surprise, from what he'd known of her before, but unusual in a virgin.

She had responded to every movement, every

touch, every kiss, so that they moved together in a perfect harmony of sensation, like long-time lovers who knew exactly how to please one another. And yet, it had been her first time. How had an untried girl managed to arouse him as no other? Was it love?

They had both spoken the words. He, at least, had meant them. He wanted to believe that she had, too. Was it love that had made it so much more than just sex?

Max had no basis of comparison, never having been in love before. For him, it had always been just sex, and there had always been incredible, often sublime, pleasure in it. With Rosalind, though, it had been something more.

Hughes was quite obviously astounded at Max's choice of wardrobe. He seldom wore anything but riding clothes in the mornings, if he dressed at all. Today, he donned a new blue tailcoat, single breasted with gilt buttons, a striped silk waistcoat, and dove-gray stirrup trousers. His shirt front was pleated, the collar points stiff and high. As tribute to his romantic mood, he achieved a perfect *trone d'amour* with his neckcloth, after only three attempts. It was, after all, a special occasion. He was going to do something he'd never done before.

He was going to ask Rosalind to marry him.

He supposed he ought to rehearse a speech or some such thing. It was a tricky situation. Rosalind might believe he was offering for her out of guilt for taking her virginity, or out of propriety because he'd compromised her, or out of honor because she might be carrying his child. Though the last reason held some validity, the other two were pure nonsense.

Max felt no guilt for what had happened. He had given her every possible opportunity to say no. For some time now, he had hoped they might eventually make love. Though he could not explain why, he also

knew in his gut that by the time the two of them finally decided to take that step, it would represent a
serious commitment. Whether it would be a commitment to marry, or simply a commitment to love, he
had not known. In fact, he had not known until this
morning, when he realized how much he wanted to
wake up beside her each day.

Rosalind's virginity was not an issue. He hadn't
been sure about it, and it had not mattered. The commitment would be there, virginity or not.

Even so, the fact that he was her first gave him an
unexpected thrill. With any other woman, it would
have terrified him. But Max had already made his decision, and the gift of her virginity only made it sweeter.

The more he thought about it, the more complicated it began to sound. It was difficult to explain
properly. Perhaps he really ought to rehearse a few
words. In the excitement of the moment, it would be
too easy to say just the wrong thing, to give the wrong
impression. Odd, for he had never been at a loss for
the right words to seduce a woman. This was not a
seduction, however, and Max wanted to do it right.
Since he'd never done it before, he really ought to
prepare something.

When Hughes had pronounced him complete to a
shade, he sat down to put his thoughts on paper.

"What the devil is going on? Where is she?"

Fanny looked up to find Max, dressed to the nines,
blowing into the room like a thundercloud. Quigley
must have told him the news. She knew exactly how
he felt, though her initial fury had given way to a
melancholy disappointment. "She's gone."

He stood quite still, stiff as a wooden soldier, and
simply stared. His mouth was set in a grim line, his
eyes flat and hard. "Am I to assume she is not simply away from home this morning," he said, his jaw

so tight he spoke through clenched teeth, "but has left London entirely?"

"She has returned to Devon, Max."

He stepped into the room and walked to the windows, turning his back to her as he gazed out at the square below. From the taut set of his shoulders and the stiff way he held his neck, she was almost glad she could not see the look on his face. Fanny had suspected for some time that Max had developed a *tendre* for the girl. After all, he had kissed her enough to make her toes curl. But that meant nothing where Max was concerned. For him, that was merely a prelude to seduction.

Good Lord, is that what had happened? Had she bolted because Max had seduced her?

"Did you know she was leaving today?" His voice was brittle and sharp, like broken glass, and his hands were balled into fists at his side. He did not turn around.

"No."

"It was not something she had planned, then?"

"Not to my knowledge."

"She just up and bolted this morning, without warning?"

"So it appears."

He slammed a fist against the window frame so hard the panes rattled in the casement. "God damn it to hell."

"Get over here and sit down, Max. I will not have you breaking my windows."

"Damn, damn, damn!"

"Max! Sit down."

He spun around and Fanny had to stifle a gasp. His face was a mask of devastation. She had thought her own despair might overwhelm her; his was apparently even more profound. Moving stiffly, as though every muscle was wound tight as a spring, he

took a seat in a chair facing the settee where Fanny sat.
If he hadn't looked so miserable, she might have boxed
his ears. She had grown fond of Rosalind, had in fact
become exceedingly attached to the girl. Fanny had thoroughly enjoyed having her about, and was going to
miss her terribly. And she suspected Max had something to do with her abrupt departure.

"What have you done, Max?"

"I beg your pardon?"

"What did you do to her?"

"I? What have *I* done?" He spat out the words an-
grily. "Better to ask what *she* has done, damn her."

"All right. What has she done?"

The anger drained from his face to be replaced by
an anguish almost painful to watch. "I don't know."
He ran a hand through his hair, disturbing the perfect waves so they fell loose over his brow. "I don't
know. But I am very much afraid, Fanny, that she has
broken my heart."

Dear God, it was worse than she'd thought. "Strange,"
she said. "I did not realize you had a heart." She smiled
so he would know she was teasing.

He did not return her smile. Instead, he said, "Neither did I."

"Oh, my dear boy." She reached out a hand, and
after a moment Max took it in his and held it tightly.

"Did you see her?" he asked.

"No. She was gone when I came downstairs. She
left a note."

"What did it say."

"That for reasons relating to her health, she was
forced to return at once to Wycombe Hall."

"Her health?"

"That is what she said." And Fanny had not believed it for a moment. Oh, perhaps for a moment,
when she recollected Sir Nigel Leighton's visit. She
had discarded the idea, however, believing something

entirely different was afoot. One look at Max and she knew she had been right.

"That's all? Nothing more?"

"And some very kind words thanking me for my hospitality, etc." Fanny had actually been quite moved by Rosalind's note. She had written how glad she was to have gotten to know Fanny, how she would always remember her with gratitude and deep affection. She would not tell Max, however, that under her signature, her niece had added a scrawled afterthought: *Please say good-bye to Max for me.* Under the circumstances—whatever they were; it was still unclear what precisely had happened—such a casual sentiment would be worse than nothing at all.

"Damn."

"She said she would write to let me know they had reached Devon safely, and would I please send along the rest of her things to Wycombe Hall at my earliest convenience."

"Damn."

"Your vocabulary has become strangely limited this morning, Max. Perhaps you should tell me what happened between you two."

He leaned down to bring to his lips the hand he still held, then released it. Sinking back in the chair, he heaved a sigh so deep it bordered on a groan. His eyes met hers and he offered a wan smile. "You will not credit it, my dear," he said, "but I actually came here today to ask Rosalind to marry me."

Fanny flinched at the impact of his words. Her jaw dropped and for a moment she could do nothing but stare at him, as if waiting for him to say he was joking. "My God," she said at last. "My God."

"Astonishing, is it not?"

"Max, darling, I had no idea. So that is why you are dressed up like a Christmas goose."

He flicked a piece of lint off his sleeve and adjusted his cravat. "I thought I looked rather fine, actually."

"Indeed you do."

He tossed his head back and looked up at the ceiling. "What a fool I am. I don't know what got into me."

"Love?"

He gave a disdainful snort. "What rot."

"Did you seduce the girl, Max?"

He sent her a baleful glance. "Not that it is any of your business, madam, but I am beginning to believe that *she* seduced me. For what purpose, I do not know. Duped me into—" He stopped and shook his head. "What a bloody fool I am."

Fanny was beginning to form a picture of what might have happened, though why the girl should have bolted was still a mystery. "Did you come to make an offer because you made love to her? Was she a virgin?"

"Dammit, Fanny—"

"Yes, of course she was. I'd wager the girl had never been outside Devon in her life before coming here." She also recalled the conversation she and her niece had had about the joys of lovemaking. There was no question Rosalind had been an innocent. "So, you were her first, and now you feel guilty and obligated to make an offer. Admirable. I confess I would never have expected it of you, Max."

"Dammit, that is *not* why I wanted to marry her."

"Oh? Then, why?"

"Because I loved her! Or thought I did."

Fanny sighed wistfully. The road to love was not always smooth. "Well then," she said, "you must go after her."

"What?"

"Max, darling, I have known you since you were a pup, and in all that time I have never known you to fall in love. If it has finally happened, surely you are not going to let her simply walk out of your life. You must go after her."

"No."

"Why?" Her hands flew up in exasperation.

"She played me for a fool, Fanny. She let me believe in something that didn't exist. I thought . . ."

"What?"

"I thought she loved me."

"Max, if that girl was not top over tail in love with you, then I'm the Queen of Sheba."

"Then why the hell did she leave?"

"I don't know!" Fanny's voice rose almost to a shriek, she was so frustrated with this stubborn, stupid man. "That is why you must go after her, to find out what you did to make her run away."

"All I did was give her exactly what she wanted. And without a word, she bolts. Right now, I swear I'm so bloody angry at her I hope I never see her again. I would not be responsible for my actions."

"Love does not simply disappear once it's got hold of you, Max."

"It doesn't have hold of me. It merely brushed against me momentarily, and now it's gone."

"Is that so?"

"Don't press, Fanny. It's over. End of story."

Fanny smiled. "We shall see."

"Oh, Papa! I'm so sorry."

Rosie clung to her father, who held her tightly in his arms. He rocked her slowly back and forth, the way he used to do when she was a child but had not done for a dozen years or more.

"My poor Rosie." His voice shook with emotion. "You thought you were going to die? Like your Mama? Why didn't you tell me? What kind of unnatural parent am I that you could not share that burden with me? Rosie, Rosie, you must have been so afraid." His voice broke and he held her tighter.

"I was, Papa," she said through her own tears. "I was terrified."

"And all alone with your pain and fear. Oh, Rosie, my heart is breaking to know how badly I failed you as a father. How I wish you could have told me. I might have spared you so much anguish. My poor girl."

She lifted her head from his shoulder and kissed his damp cheek. "I wish I had told you, too, Papa, but I just could not."

He reached in his coat pocket and retrieved a handkerchief, then gently dabbed at her wet face and eyes. "I have not been a good father to you, Rosie. It pains me to realize how far I've slipped away from my own children, so far that they can no longer confide in me. The one person in your life who ought to have been there to support you was not there. I've failed you, daughter, and I do not know what I can ever do to make it up to you."

"Oh, Papa."

"I've failed you in every possible way. I've taken advantage of you, relied on you for everything since your Mama died. I just always assumed you'd be there to take care of things. But I've learned a thing or two since you left. I've learned how much you do for Wycombe, and for me and all your brothers and sisters. You're the rock upon which this family is built. That role ought to have been mine, but I abdicated it to you. It shames me to admit that by doing so, I caused you to miss everything a girl should experience in life."

Rosie sent him a sheepish grin. "I think I've more than made up for anything I may have missed."

He stroked her cheek and smiled. "I'm glad you had such a good time."

Her expression clouded. "But Papa, I told you how

it was. I did terrible, shameful things. Things no re-spectable young lady should do."

She had told him everything, or almost everything, relating all the details of her perfidy in a dispassion-ate voice, while inside she burned with humiliation. He had listened patiently, letting her finish before he spoke. In the end, though, he had been more affected by her belief in her imminent death than by any es-capade she recounted. "Are you not angry with me?"

"No, Rosie, I am not. I am too angry with myself to begrudge you a bit of fun."

"But Papa, I am so ashamed. I only did those things because I was pretending to be someone I am not. I was fearless and reckless and wild, not at all my true self."

"I wouldn't be so sure of that. When you were a child, you were as fearless and reckless as they come. More than any of your brothers and sisters. You were vivacious and happy and outgoing." He looked over her shoulder and tapped his chin with a finger. "Funny. I'd forgotten that. I always think of you as quiet, efficient, sensible Rosie. But you were quite dif-ferent as a child. Before your mother died. I suspect it was your old true self that rose to the surface in London. I'm glad. You deserve a bit of frivolity after all these quiet years."

"Oh, I was frivolous, Papa. And worse." She took a deep breath and expelled it through puffed cheeks. "There was a man, Papa."

He arched a brow. "Oh?"

"He is a friend of Aunt Fanny's. His name is Max Davenant and he is an infamous rake."

"Are you in love with this man?"

"Yes, but that is not the point. I . . . I became very much involved with him."

"I see," he said, and fixed his gaze on hers for sev-eral long moments. "Is there to be a child?"

She chewed on her lip, contemplating how to answer him. Finally, she simply said, "I don't know." Pain and sadness gathered in his eyes at the implication of her words, and she had to look away. "I thought I would be dead soon. I didn't think . . ." Her throat closed up and she could say no more. Tears pooled on her lashes and spilled down her cheeks. She could not bear to think how much she had hurt him.

"Well," he said, "we shall just have to wait and see. Whatever you decide to do, Rosie, you have my full support. I have failed you for too long, but no longer. In this matter, it shall be just as you wish. If you love this man and want to marry him, you have my blessing. If he is not willing to do the right thing, then I will do whatever is necessary to convince him otherwise."

"I cannot marry Max, Papa."

His brows knit into a frown. "Why not?"

"He believes I am someone else."

Chapter 13

"I am not going after her."

"But Max, darling—"

"No!" He wished she would just leave him alone. Fanny had been singing the same tune for a week, and it was growing tiresome. "Eldridge, take her away, will you? Is there not someone else she can harass for a while?"

"Come along, my dear," Lord Eldridge said, taking Fanny's elbow. "The company is thin tonight. Let us go home and find better company." He gave her a rakish leer and she grinned like a young girl as she was gently steered toward the exit.

Lord, but she must have been a siren when she was young. No wonder his father had loved her. But at the moment, Max was heartily sick of her. He had stopped visiting Berkley Square, in hopes of avoiding her, but he saw her everywhere else. He had not even considered curtailing his usual activities. The last thing he wanted was to make a public statement of his broken heart, so he continued to make appearances at all the best parties and balls. Unfortunately, Fanny often attended the same events, and she made a point of tracking him down and haranguing him about Rosalind.

Max did not need Fanny's prodding. He could not stop thinking about Rosalind, puzzling over her departure. One moment he hated her passionately, the next he relived their love-making in all its sweet detail and fell in love with her all over again.

He had told Fanny that Rosalind had broken his heart. Max had a new respect for that old cliché. Whoever coined the phrase must have felt just as Max did. The pain of loss was almost physical in its intensity and centered in the area of the chest. It hurt so badly it did indeed feel as though something inside him was broken.

The worst part was not knowing why. If he at least knew why she had left, maybe it would hurt a little less.

Once or twice, he even considered taking Fanny's advice and going to Devon—not to sweep her into his arms and carry her away, but only to find out what the devil had happened. He did not believe it was a coincidence that she left London only hours after sharing his bed; but he did not know what the hell it meant.

"I say, Davenant, heard your little bird has flown the coop."

Oh, God. "If you are speaking of Miss Lacey, Overton, you are correct. She has returned to her home in the country."

"How very interesting," the blond devil said. "What do you suppose prompted her to leave?"

"I have no idea. Perhaps you should ask her aunt."

He plucked absently at the lace at his cuffs, adjusting the fall. "As it happens, I did."

"And what did she say?"

"Some mumbo-jumbo about her health," Overton said. "But that's what they always say, is it not, when an unmarried girl needs to disappear for some months. They go off to some continental spa to take the waters, and return with an infant left to them by some unnamed relative, or adopted off the street, or some such tarradiddle."

Max hung onto his temper by a thin thread. "I trust, Overton, that you are not spreading such a fiction about Miss Lacey," he said, his voice edged with steel. "It would be a most ungentlemanly thing to do."

"Egad, I hope you are not threatening me, Davenant," Overton drawled as his gaze surveyed the ballroom with lazy disinterest. "She is a prime article, to be sure, but not worthy of an affair of honor, don't you agree?"

"Don't push me, Overton. I'm in a foul mood and just itching to blow off some steam."

The cad held up his hands in a gesture of mock defense. "You terrify me. I would not dream of risking an insult, I assure you. Ah, I see Lady Gwedolyn Haskill has arrived," he said, and lifted his quizzing glass to study the young woman's entrance. "I do hope she is not another of your protégées, Davenant. I've already had her, too, you see." He walked away with a fluid catlike grace that set Max's teeth on edge.

God, how he wanted to plant the man a facer. And he would, if the blackguard started to circulate salacious hints about Rosalind's departure. Max was still furious at Rosalind, but he had no wish for malicious rumors to be spread about her.

The truth was, of course, that such rumors might ultimately prove to be true. She might indeed be carrying his child. Every time he pondered that particular notion, he had to stop himself from jumping into the fastest carriage he could find and rushing off to Devon to discover the truth. If she was pregnant, it was *his* child. It could be no one else's. And if she carried his child, he wanted to know about it, had a right to know about it.

It had only been a week since they'd made love. She couldn't possibly know yet if she was pregnant. Could she? If he was going to go haring off to Devon, he wanted to return with answers. He would wait until a month had passed, then, if he had not heard from her, he would go to her father's estate and confront her. If she was pregnant, then by God she would marry him. If she wasn't, he would return to London and try to forget her.

That, however, would be difficult. Before they'd made love, he had told Rosalind he thought it would be unforgettable, and so it had been. Sweet and passionate and unforgettable.

Forgetting her was impossible. He would simply have to learn to live without her.

"So, it's true what she said?" Sir Edmund asked his son. "She really did do all those things?"

Thomas squirmed in his seat and looked thoroughly uncomfortable. He had returned from London earlier that afternoon, obviously concerned about Rosie and relieved to find her safe and well. Sir Edmund had called his son into the library and told him the truth of his mother's death. Keeping the epilepsy a secret had done too much damage to his family. There would be no more secrets. Now, if only he could become a better father to his children.

"Well, son?"

Thomas cleared his throat. "She . . . she was quite popular, sir."

Sir Edmund smiled. "I knew she would be. Pretty as her mother. I like her new short hair, though I must say it took me by surprise."

"It is all the crack," Thomas said. "Every woman in town wanted to emulate her style. Ought to have seen her all put together for a ball. Bang up to the nines, she was. I almost didn't recognize her. She looked . . . beautiful."

"I suppose Fanny had more than a little to do with it. Always had flair, my sister."

"Aunt Fanny is still a very handsome woman."

"Is she? Haven't seen her in years. Tell me, son, did you actually see any of these antics of your sister?"

"Antics, sir?" He was squirming again.

"Settle down, Thomas, I'm not angry with Rosie and I'm not asking you to reveal any secrets. It is just so . . . so difficult to imagine our Rosie racing a curricle through Hyde Park."

Thomas sent his father a lop-sided grin, and seemed to be more at ease. "Actually, she did that several times," he said. "Quite a whip, our Rosie. Saw her race Lady Kirby from Holbourn to Hampstead. Won, too."

"And is it true that she ripped up at old Talmadge?"

"Smack in the middle of the Royal Academy exhibition with half the *ton* looking on," Thomas said, beaming with pride. "Can't blame her for that, sir. High time somebody told him what's what."

Sir Edmund chuckled. "Good old Rosie. Hard to imagine."

"She was different, sir. Not the quiet, prim girl we're all accustomed to. She was . . . I don't know . . . vibrant. Dynamic. Different."

"I'd like to have seen that."

Thomas pulled a face. "She's back to the old Rosie, ain't she?"

"Seems to be. Except for the hair, of course."

"A shame. She cut quite a dash in town."

"Lots of beaux?"

"Dozens."

Sir Edmund's brows shot up to his hairline. "Really?"

"Lord, you would not have believed it, sir. Every rake, rogue, buck, beau, and blood in town was dangling after her. She had a whole circle of 'em around her everywhere she went."

"Did she? No one in particular? She mentioned some fellow . . . Davenant, I think."

"Max Davenant. Greatest rake in London. List of conquests as long as your arm."

"Oh?" And his little Rosie was one of them, damn the man's eyes.

"He's a friend of Fanny's. I daresay that's how Rosie got to know him."

"Davenant. Where have I heard—Wait a moment. Davenant. That's the name of the Earl of Blythe, is it not?"

"Yes. Max, I believe, is one of the younger brothers of the present earl."

And the son of Fanny's lover, Basil Davenant. Sir Edmund wondered if perhaps Fanny had set this up deliberately: his daughter with her lover's son. It would appeal to her sense of irony.

"Tell me about this Max Davenant. What sort of fellow is he, besides being a rake?"

"He's a first-rate player. Amazing luck. Saw him one night with R—er, with friends, and he was having the most incredible streak at the hazard table. Superb ivory-turner."

A rake *and* a gambler? Good Lord, what had Rosie done? "Sounds like a rough character to me."

"Oh no, sir. Straight as an arrow. Never heard any whispers of him running the legs off young gulls or taking some poor sod's estate. Not a Greek. Nothing like that."

"What about women?"

"Even more luck there, I should say. The man's deuced good-looking and oozes charm, if you take my meaning. But nothing havey-cavey as far as I know. Sticks to high flyers. Never heard of him ruining young innocents or anything of that sort."

Until now. Poor old Rosie. She would have been particularly vulnerable to that sort of seducer. So innocent for her age, so anxious to explore all she could in the short time she believed was left her. His heart still ached to think of that fateful misapprehension.

"An adventurer?" he asked.

"No, sir. No need to be. Seems to have a tidy fortune. Oh, I say. Got a picture of him and Rosie." Thomas reached deep into a pocket and finally extracted a slightly crumpled piece of paper. "Rosie won't be pleased, but take a look, sir."

Sir Edmund did, and burst out laughing. "Well, I'm dashed. Suppose I have to believe it now, don't I? My little Rosie made famous, and buxom, by Mr. Rowlandson. And this fine, broad fellow with the lantern jaw is your good-looking gamester?"

"His jaw is exaggerated, just like Rosie's bos—well, you know. But the cravat is spot on. Perfect mathematical."

"I think I should like to know more about this Davenant fellow."

"Why?"

"Curiosity. I do believe it's time I wrote my sister."

"Did you really waltz without permission?" Pamela's expression was a combination of incredulity and awe. Though never as stiff-necked as Ursula, she still maintained conventional notions of propriety. During her own Season, Pamela would have died before breaking one of the accepted rules of ladylike behavior.

"I'm afraid it's true," Rosie said. They sat together on a stone bench in Wycombe's rose garden. Rosie breathed deeply of the lush fragrance of hundreds of blossoms and tried to convince herself that this quiet, pastoral life was what she wanted. It was. It always had been. She loved Wycombe. If only memories of London didn't intrude at random moments, unsettling her peace and tranquility. It would be easier to forget about her London adventures if she was not constantly queried about them.

Pamela giggled, reminding Rosie that her sister was only nineteen—still a young, giddy girl, despite marriage and impending motherhood. Pamela had always been the least restrained of the three sisters. A chatterbox from the age of two, she always had something to say on every subject. Today, her subject of interest was Rosie's adventure in London.

"Oh, Rosie, I can hardly believe you did all those things. Not you! It's . . . it's . . ."

"Outrageous?"

"Yes! And I hope you won't repeat this to Ursula or Papa, but I think it's wonderful that you kicked up your heels. I wish I could have been there!"

"You would not have been pleased with me, Pam. Quite the opposite I should think."

"Tommy says you were magnificent, that Aunt Fanny turned you out in fine rig. I do like your short hair. It is so much more becoming than your old style. Do you think I should have mine cut?"

Pamela was the only blonde in the family, and her golden ringlets had always been the envy of her sisters. "Your hair is always lovely, Pam. You must do as you please. Thomas is right, though. If I had any style at all, it was due to Fanny. I don't believe I have a fashionable bone in my body."

"I cannot wait for your trunks to arrive so you can show us your gowns."

Rosie did not know what she was going to do with all her new clothes. None of them suited country life and certainly did not suit Rosie. They had belonged to Rosalind.

"Thomas also says you had a bigger circle of admirers than any other girl. Is that true?"

Dear God, she wished they could talk of something else. "There were several gentlemen who were very kind to me. Have you and John thought of names for the baby yet?"

"There's plenty of time for that. How many gentlemen?"

"What?"

"How many gentlemen in your circle? Last year, when I was out, Miranda Fenimore had more beaux than anyone and the rest of us were green with envy. She never had fewer than seven or eight gentlemen paying court to her. Did you have as many as that?"

"I don't remember."

"Rosie! Don't be so tiresome. I'm dying to know everything. It is so exciting to have my own sister cut such a dash. Who were some of your beaux?"

Rosie gave a weary sigh. "I don't believe I had any beaux." Except one, and she would *not* speak of him. "I had a lot of friends and acquaintances, that is all."

Pamela scowled in exasperation. "You are going to make me pull out every detail one at a time, aren't you? All right then. Did you drive in the park with any gentlemen?"

"Yes."

"Who?"

"Pamela!"

"Name one. Just one gentlemen who drove you in the park."

"Jeremy Aldrich."

"Hmm, I think I may have met him once, but I cannot be certain. Who else?"

"You said just one."

"Please, Rosie. Someone I might know of."

"Lord Radcliffe."

"You rode with Lord Radcliffe? Goodness, Rosie, but isn't he a rake? Lady Hartwell would not allow me to associate with him. He is quite handsome, though, is he not? And who else?"

"Enough, Pamela."

"Oh, don't be such a bore. If you are worried that I will tell Ursula that you consorted with rakes, I promise I will not."

"I am much obliged to you, I'm sure. Why don't you tell me about your plans for the nursery. Have you chosen a nurse yet? Do you think Mrs. Theobald will be available?"

"We can talk about all that later. Were there any other rakes in your circle? No, don't give me that look. How about . . . let's see . . . Mr. Dwight Newcombe. Did you drive out with him or dance with him?"

"Yes."

"Did you? Two rakes, Rosie? Let me see if I can recall any others. How about Mr. Alfred Hepworth?"

"Yes."

"Oh, my! Three. And Lord Vaughn?"

"Yes."

Pamela squealed with delight. "Four! I cannot believe it. Did no one tell you these gentlemen were rakes, Rosie? No, of course not. Aunt Fanny no doubt encouraged them. That is just the sort of gentleman she prefers, I suspect."

"Please do not disparage my aunt. You do not know her, Pam. She is the most wonderful woman I ever met. If I chose to keep company with a less than respectable set of gentlemen, that was my own doing, not hers. She let me do exactly as I pleased. Every shocking thing I did was my own decision. Now I have to live with my horrid behavior. It is not something of which I am very proud. I would prefer to forget about it, if you please."

"What about Lord Bigelow?"

"Pamela!"

"Was he one of your circle? He was a great flirt, as I recall, but I do not know if he would be considered a rake, precisely."

"I do not believe I met him."

"Never met him? Hmm. Who else? Oh, and there is Lord Overton. We were all most particularly warned about him. Did you meet him?"

"Briefly," she said through clenched teeth. "I only danced with him once."

Pamela clapped her hands and bounced with glee. "Famous! I will wager you even knew Max Davenant, the most notorious rake of them all and as handsome a man as you're ever likely to meet. Except for my John, of course. Mr. Davenant stayed away from young girls like me, though. But you are so much older. Did you meet him, too? Was he another one of your rakes?"

Rosie stood up and walked toward one of the lattice-work arbors. Her hands were shaking. She had so hoped his name would not come up. "I'd like to go inside now. I believe I have the headache. I think I'd like to lie down for a while."

Pamela came and put an arm around Rosie's shoulder. "I'm sorry. I should not have pressed you. If you really do not wish to talk about London, then I will trouble you no more. But you cannot blame me for being interested. It all sounds so exciting. And so unlike you. I mean, Rosie, you are such a quiet, reserved sort of person. Not at all the sort one would associate with rakes and high jinks and who knows what else. It is fascinating because it doesn't sound at all like you. What possessed you?"

"I don't know, Pam. Some demon from hell, I daresay. I just wish it had never happened, and I do not want to talk about it any more."

"All right, Rosie. I'm sorry I've made you sad. Perhaps one day you will tell me everything. In the meantime, I will ask no more."

At least there was one thing she need never tell. Rosie was not pregnant. She wished she had waited before telling Papa. He might never have had to know.

Instead, he would never be able to look at her in the same way. In his eyes, despite his kind words, she would always be ruined.

A tear rolled down her cheek and she pondered how grief was just as powerful, even when the thing lost had never existed.

Chapter 14

"This had better be important." Max had received an urgent note from Fanny, asking him to come to Berkley Square at once. "If this is about Rosalind—"

"Sit down, Max, and try not to glower."

He entered the sitting room and took his customary seat, keeping a wary eye on Fanny. He crossed one leg languidly over the other, tugged at the ends of his waistcoat, flicked a piece of lint off his sleeve, and lifted an expectant brow.

"Now, don't eat me, Max. It is about Rosalind."

He shot to his feet and headed toward the door. By Jove, he'd had enough.

"Wait, Max. I've had a letter from Edmund. I think you'd better hear what he has to say."

Max halted in the doorway. Would this be the explanation he'd wanted? Was he finally to learn the truth regarding Rosalind's sudden departure?

He turned slowly to face Fanny. His stomach tied itself into knots of tension. After all the uncertainty, he was almost afraid to discover the truth. He walked back into the room and resumed his seat. "Well? What does he say?"

Fanny smiled and a softness in her eyes gave him cause to hope. "It is quite extraordinary, really," she said. "One doesn't know whether to laugh or cry, it was all so ludicrous. I'm afraid it's a long story."

"Then you had better begin."

She breathed a little sigh and met his gaze squarely. "A few months back, Rosalind developed symptoms that resembled those her mother had experienced before her death. The details do not matter. Suffice it to say that a quack doctor confirmed Rosalind's own diagnosis and led her to believe she had only a few months to live."

Oh, God. She really had been ill? A jolt of fear shot through him like an electrical charge. Was she going to die? Oh, God.

"For reasons only she can explain, Rosalind did not tell anyone of her presumed fate. Instead, she decided to use the last months of her life to ... to do all the things she'd always wanted to do. She meant to cram a lifetime of living into a few short months."

"Her list!"

"Yes. It was not simply a list of sights and events and activities to be found in London. It was a list ..." Her voiced cracked a little and she took a breath to compose herself. "It was a list of all the things she wanted to do before she died."

"Dear God. No wonder she seemed so hungry for experience, so open to any new idea or suggestion." Fanny had been right. He didn't know whether to laugh or cry. There was something pathetic and sad about such a list. But there was also a sort of cock-eyed logic to it that seemed uniquely Rosalind.

Fanny brushed at her eyes but kept a smile in place. "It also explains why she thumbed her nose at convention. It didn't matter to her. Why bother to maintain a respectable reputation when she would not be around to enjoy it? The truly sad part is that the poor girl carried around all that pain and fear without telling a single soul. Except—"

"Leighton."

"Just so. Apparently she thought it wise to consult

a London physician, in case her condition worsened and she needed help. He was able to wheedle from her the name of her mother's physician. He discovered two things. First, her mother's condition had not been hereditary and Rosalind did not suffer from it. Second, the symptoms she had suffered were the result of some sort of poisoning of the water in a nearby stream. A temporary reaction, not fatal."

"She is not going to die, then?"

"Not for many long years, I hope."

Max expelled a pent-up breath in a long, shuddery sigh. "Thank God."

"Sir Nigel wrote to tell her his discovery. She received his letter when she returned home—from your bed?—the night before she left."

"Are you saying she left because of his letter? I do not understand."

"I'm not sure I do either, but then neither of us was inside her mind to know what nonsense she was thinking. All Edmund says is that she is mortified at all she did here, the name she made for herself, the reputation she earned for being a bit wild, a little fast, up for anything. She could not face all she'd done, and went home to hide."

Max could no longer suppress a smile. "Fanny! Is that it? That's why she left?"

"Apparently."

"Ha!" He jumped to his feet, unable to contain the sudden burst of jubilant energy that charged through his body. "The little fool!" He began to laugh—for joy that she had not rejected him for some more credible reason, for the absurdity of her reaction to learning she was going to live, for hope that he might still be able to marry her. "You were right, Fanny, she had indeed been in my bed that night, and now she must believe she is ruined. Ha! If only she had stayed a few more hours she would have had my offer. She is not ruined. She is simply cork-brained."

"And are you finally going to go after her, then?"

"Of course I am! I love the little idiot."

"Max, darling, I am so pleased. Edmund asked about you, by the way. Quite a lot of questions about you."

Max arched a brow. "He did?"

"Rosalind confessed everything to him. *Everything*."

"Egad. Is he preparing to come after me with a gun, to force me into marriage with her?" Max grinned so hard his face hurt. "He needn't bother. I'll be there with bells on."

"He only asked about your character, not about your intentions."

"I trust you will paint a glowing picture of me, my dear, leaving out all the sordid bits, of course."

"I will tell him you are a handsome, intelligent, honorable man who has waited his whole life to find the right woman, and has finally found her in Rosalind. I will tell him that though you can be a tad stubborn—after all, you could have learned this whole story weeks ago if only you'd followed her to Devon—on the whole, you are a marvelous man."

Max grabbed her and hugged her tight. "Thank you, my dear. Rosalind is not the only woman in my life. I love you too, Fanny."

"Darling boy."

Max was glad he'd decided to ride the entire way to Wycombe. He made better time, and it allowed him to work off the excess energy that would continue to keep him on edge until he finally saw her again.

When he reached Upper Wycombe, he had stopped at an inn to clean up before presenting himself to Rosalind. With Wycombe Hall in sight just beyond the copse, he was itching to ride hell for leather to the front door. But, vain creature that he was, Max did not want to undo all he had done to make himself presentable. Even without Hughes to help, Max was quite sure he looked an exquisite picture of manly perfection: claret coat, blue embroidered waistcoat, buff breeches, and gleeming top boots.

He swung down from the saddle and began to walk. He'd had several days on the road to compose what he would say to Rosalind, and he went over the words again as he approached the house.

"Hullo! What's a flash cove like you doing at Wycombe?"

Max stopped and looked around but saw no one.

"Capital neckcloth. Mathematical, ain't it?"

The same voice from a different direction. What the devil?

"Don't be daft, Robbie, it's an oriental."

Two voices?

"Up here, mister."

Max looked up to find a lanky boy of about thirteen or fourteen perched on a tree limb about eight feet above the left side of the lane. His curly chestnut hair and generous mouth marked him as a relation of Rosalind's. "Good afternoon," Max said. "And whom do I have the honor of addressing? Mr. Lacey, perhaps?"

"Right you are, sir. How'd you know? We ain't met, have we?"

"I do not believe I've had the pleasure. My name is Davenant."

"How d'you do? I'm Robert Lacey at your service." He bowed from the waist without losing his balance. "And over there—" he pointed across the lane to another boy perched on a limb "—is m'brother David."

Max turned to the second boy and swept a bow. The two were as alike as buttons on a topcoat. "I am pleased to meet you both. And you are correct, David, this is an oriental."

"Ha! Told you, Robbie. Say, do you know my brother, Thomas?"

"We have met."

"Thought so. Recognized the name. Hey, Robbie, this here gent is the ivory-turner Tommy told us about. Prime player, he says. You coming to visit Tommy? Would you teach us to play hazard?"

"Actually, I've come to see your sister, Rosalind."

"Rosie?" This was from Robert. "What you want to see her for?"

"We have a bit of unfinished business."

"You and Rosie?" Robert said. "What's a swell like you want with her?"

Max smiled. Like most brothers, they did not appreciate the finer points of their sister. "I'm afraid it is a private matter," he said.

"She went up to London a while back," David said. "Is that where you know her from?"

"Yes, it is. I say, fellows, could you do a chap a favor and hop down to ground level? My neck's growing stiff."

With identical lanky grace, the boys scrambled down from their respective perches and jumped to the ground. The Laceys were a tall family. These young cubs were almost as tall as Max. "I am much obliged, gentlemen. Now, perhaps you can tell me where I might find Rosalind at this time of day. Will she be up at the house?"

"Never heard anybody call her Rosalind," David said. "Sounds kind of funny. She's just plain old Rosie to us."

"I daresay you will find her in the herb garden," Robert said. "She'll be gathering plants and such for the still room. We can take you there."

"I would appreciate it," Max said. They led the way

and he followed, walking alongside the hired horse, a skittish little mare who seemed anxious to do more than trot along at a sedate pace.

"Still don't get it," David said. At least Max thought it was David. "Can't imagine what sort of business you have with Rosie."

"He already said it was private, Davey. Stubble it."

"Hold on," David said, turning around to walk backward and fixing his gaze on Max. "You ain't . . . what d'you call it? . . . coming to pay your addresses?"

"Don't be daft, Davey. Nobody comes to court Rosie. She ain't that type of female."

"Yes, she is," Max said, and grinned when both boys stopped dead in their tracks.

"Rosie?" they said in squeaky unison.

"Gentlemen, you obviously do not realize what a remarkable sister you have."

"You're right there," Robert said.

"Do you know," Max said, "when she was in London, she was the most sought-after female in town?"

"Rosie?" Again, two voices in unison.

"Yes, Rosie." Max was thoroughly enjoying their stunned disbelief. "Devilish good sport, up to any rig. Your sister was more fun than any woman ever to visit the Metropolis."

"Now, there you're out, sir," Robert said. "Can't possibly mean our Rosie. Got her confused with some other female."

"Must have. She ain't exactly the fun-loving type."

"Good sort of sister and all, but dull as ditch water and about as much fun."

"Always busy doing things, looking out for everyone. Never one to go on a lark or get into a scrape."

"Rosie's what you might call a sensible sort of female. A bit prim around the edges, if you get my meaning."

"And she ain't exactly young, you know. Couldn't

be. Our Mama died when we were two and Rosie raised us. She's way too old to have beaux."

"Got the wrong female, sir. Must have."

Max had lost track of who was who in this fascinating recital of their sister's character. He wondered if the twins' perception of Rosalind was typical of the rest of her family, perhaps even of the neighborhood. It would certainly go far in explaining her current mortification over her London behavior.

"I believe I have the right person," Max said. "Miss Rosalind Lacey of Wycombe Hall, sister to Mr. Thomas Lacey."

"Gad, sir, I daresay you've been taken in. But there's the herb garden, just down the path, and that's her with the basket."

"I am once again obliged, gentlemen. Perhaps we will have another opportunity to chat later."

"I'd give a monkey to learn how to tie an oriental like that."

"Stubble it, Davey. You ain't even got a monkey."

"I should be happy to offer what advice I can," Max said. "But first, I must speak with your sister. In private. Could I impose once again and ask that you take my horse to the stables? Thank you, gentlemen. Until we meet again, your servant."

Max watched them walk away, heads bent together, commiserating, no doubt, on the strange case of mistaken identity. What a pair. And Rosie had been a little mother to them. No wonder she had never had time for a Season or anything else . . . until there was only one last Season left to her. Or so she'd thought.

She did not see him approach, so he had time to study her. He almost began to believe the twins had been right. Could this be Rosalind, in a shapeless brown stuff dress and hideous straw bonnet?

He had to see her face. He stepped inside the garden gate. The sound alerted her and she turned to face him. She let out a gasp and dropped her basket.

Dear God, what had happened to her? Beneath the ugly bonnet, her color was wan, her eyes sunken and framed in dark circles, her cheeks were drawn, and her mouth pulled down into a frown. Where was the vibrant, radiant, beautiful woman he'd known in London?

"Rosalind?"

Why had he come? She wished he hadn't. It made it so much worse, to have him see her here, like this. At least now he will know without question that she was not Rosalind. She was not his minx. Maybe he would develop such a disgust for her that he would go away and never come back. She hoped so.

"Rosalind, my love." He stepped toward her, arms outstretched.

Oh God, how she wanted to fall into his embrace. But she could not, would not. Why did he have to come here? She stepped back and made a gesture for him to stay away.

"Why are you here, Max?" She was surprised at the even tone of her voice. Her insides were quaking.

He looked so devastatingly handsome. He smiled, and those heavy-lidded eyes reminded her of last time she'd seen him. He had been sleeping, naked, beside her. "I thought you'd run away because of something I did, that I had hurt you somehow."

"Oh no, Max, it was not that. Never that."

"I have just learned why you left."

"You have?"

"Yes, and it gives me hope that you do not despise me."

"I could never despise you."

His soft smile broadened. "I am exceedingly glad to hear it. And so I have come here, ridden all the

way, just to say to you now what I came to say to
you at Fanny's that next day. But you were gone, and
my heart was broken."

Just as hers was breaking now. Please don't say it,
she silently pleaded. Don't say those words again,
those words that are meant for someone else.

"Our night together was pure magic," he said. "So
much so that I want to spend every night for the rest
of my life with you in my arms. I came to Fanny's
the very next morning to tell you that, and to ask you
to be my wife."

Rosie's hands flew to her cheeks in horror. "Oh
no."

"Oh yes, minx. If you hadn't bolted, you would
have heard my impassioned offer. I was so disappointed you weren't there to receive me. I had dressed
most particularly for the occasion, you see. Fanny told
me I looked like a Christmas goose."

"Max."

"You really did break my heart, you know." His
expression grew more serious. "When I learned why
you left—"

"How did you find out?"

"Your father wrote to Fanny and she told me."

"Oh." She might have expected it, though Papa had
not communicated with Fanny in years. She supposed
her aunt deserved to know why she left. Now that
she did know, Rosie would write herself and try to
explain.

"I cannot, of course, know what you must have felt."
His dark eyes studied her intently as he spoke. "But I
would wager that our night together was high on the
list of transgressions plaguing your conscience. When
we made love, you did it freely and willingly and without concern for the consequences. Perhaps that's one
of the reasons it was so special. You were able to completely abandon yourself to pleasure. Leighton's reve-

lations must have shaken you to the core, to suddenly realize there might be consequences after all. You were ruined. You might be pregnant."

"I am not pregnant." Her voice sounded thin and strangled.

"No?" He regarded her thoughtfully and a hint of sadness flickered in his eyes. "I'm so sorry."

Her brows rose at the note of sincerity in his voice.

"I would not have minded, Rosalind. In fact . . . in fact, I think I should have been very pleased." He looked as if the idea took him by surprise. A smile tugged at the corner of his lips. "But there will be many other opportunities, my minx, when we are married. If you will have me, that is. Will you marry me, Rosalind?"

He still did not understand. He thought nothing had changed. "No, Max."

He flinched as though she'd slapped him. "No?"

"No. I'm sorry, Max."

"Rosalind." He reached out for her hand. She pulled away, but he grabbed her and held her in a tight grip. "I thought you loved me," he said. "You know that I love you. I told you so, over and over as I recall."

"In the heat of passion."

"Passion, desire, love. It all became one."

"You told me once that you often fell in love in the heat of passion, but that it always passed."

"Not this time. That's one of the reasons I know it is real. I haven't held you in my arms in three weeks and I'm still hopelessly in love with you."

"With someone else, not me."

"What?"

"The woman you fell in love with does not exist. She was a role and I was the actress. It was all a pretense, a part I played for a brief time. But it was not real. It was not me. This is me." She swept her free hand over the drab brown dress and apron. "I am not Rosalind. I never was. I've always been just plain Rosie."

He loosened his grip and entwined his fingers with hers. "My dear girl, you may have thought you were playing a part, but you cannot have been acting the whole time. I daresay some of your actions may have been pretense; after all, you had nothing to lose by being as outrageous as you pleased. But the vibrant, radiant core driving all those actions came from you."

"Max, I—"

"You may have had to reach deep inside just plain Rosie to find it, but the spark was there. It had to be, my dear. You could not have done it otherwise."

She jerked her hand free. "You're wrong, Max. You have no idea how easy it is to don a mask when you think you are dying. When one has no future to answer to, it is remarkable how flexible one's character becomes. I suppose it is akin to someone unaccustomed to spirits becoming thoroughly inebriated, with total loss of inhibition and judgment. But inebriation is temporary. Death is not. There was nothing to stop me from being anyone I wanted, so I became the dashing Rosalind."

He offered an indulgent, almost patronizing smile, as though he did not believe her. "It pains me, Max, to know you fell in love with Rosalind. I am more sorry than you'll ever know. But she is gone."

"She is not. I am looking at her."

"At Rosie."

"What's in a name? Rosie, Rosalind, Ross—I'll call you by any name you want. You're still the woman I love, no matter what you may think."

"No, I—"

"Yes! Yes, you are, Rosie. Do you know how special you are to me? Do you know that I never once in all my life told a woman I loved her? Until you. And you know my history. You know how many women have been in my life. Doesn't it mean anything to you that you are the first, the first and only?"

"It only makes it harder, knowing that. I'm sorry, Max."

"There has always been something eternal about the whole concept of love that frightened me. I never allowed any relationship with a woman to endure for fear it would change my life, my selfish, pleasure-seeking existence. Well, by Jove, it *has* changed my life. *You* have changed my life, and I am forever grateful to you for it. Did you know I was ready to end my life before I met you?"

"What?"

"I had become tired and bored beyond measure, and planned to put a bullet in my head at the end of the Season. But then you came into my life and made me want to live again."

The blackguard. He was being overly dramatic, hoping to play on her sympathy. Well, she wasn't buying. Max commit suicide? Never. "And you think life with me, with *Rosie*, would relieve your boredom, your fatal ennui? I am a country person, Max, with country notions. Shall I tell you what life here is like? I get up early because there is so much to do, and go to bed early because there is nothing to do—no parties, routs, balls, operas. We fall asleep after dinner out of sheer tedium. It is quiet and uneventful, thoroughly humdrum. The highlight of the week is meeting the neighbors after church on Sunday to critique the vicar's sermon, compare crop yields, and exchange recipes. There hasn't been a scandal in the neighborhood since the time of Charles II. This is my milieu, Max, my real life. I am a product of this world and a part of it. I belong here, not in the glittering world of London."

"I grew up in the country, too," he said. "I even own a little farm in Suffolk and a hunting box in the shires. But a country upbringing never kept me from enjoying London or any other place."

"I have had my adventure in London, and it brought me nothing but shame and guilt. I can never belong to your world, Max."

He took her hand once again. "But you did once. And you can do it again."

"No. I'm sorry. I cannot be the woman you want me to be. I cannot marry you, Max."

"Will you think about it a bit longer? My visit has surprised you, caught you off guard. You do not need to give me an answer right now. I have a room at the King's Head and will stay as long as you want. We can spend time together, get to know one another again." He brought her hand to his lips. "Give me a chance, Rosie."

Chapter 15

"You confound me, sir." Rosie's father was near to wearing a path in the Turkey carpet as he paced back and forth in front of the library windows. "All I knew of you before today was that you were a rake of the first order who'd taken my daughter's virtue." He stopped and looked at Max. "Or is it more accurate to say she gave it away?"

"Despite her belief that there would be no consequences to her actions," Max said, "Rosalind was no wanton, Sir Edmund. She engaged in one or two playful flirtations, but she did not discard all judgment, regardless of what she may now believe. She came to my bed willingly, but I do not think she made the decision lightly."

"My sister, who takes a lot of the blame for what happened upon herself, believes losing her virginity was just another thing Rosie wanted to do before she died."

Max could not suppress a smile. "It's quite possible. She did have a list."

Sir Edmund chucked softly. "That's my Rosie. Efficient and organized to a fault. She's kept this place running smoothly for years with her lists. So she wants to experience physical love before she dies, and has the good fortune to have an accommodating rake at hand. An easy conquest for you, I daresay."

"No, sir," Max said. "It was in fact the most difficult decision of my life."

Sir Edmund lifted a skeptical brow. "Because she was a virgin?"

"No. Because I loved her. I would not have made love to your daughter, Sir Edmund, without believing I was making a commitment to her by doing so."

"Persuasive words. They must come easy to a practiced seducer."

Max looked at the man earnestly, willing him to believe what he said. "I am sure it must seem that way, knowing the sort of life I've led. I've made a career of seducing women. But I tell you quite frankly, sir, your daughter complicated that career by turning my world upside down. It is the first time in all my long years of pleasure-seeking that I have fallen in love. I want to marry her, Sir Edmund, but she won't have me."

Sir Edmund gave a little start of surprise. "Why?"

"Says she is not the girl I knew in London. Says it was all play-acting, not real. The woman I fell in love with, she tells me, does not exist. That is why I have come to you, Sir Edmund. I need your help to make her see how wrong she is."

"Damnation." Sir Edmund started to pace again, his hands behind his back. After a long pensive moment, he said, "She's running scared."

"I beg your pardon?"

"Let us have a glass of claret, Davenant, while I tell you about my daughter."

Sir Edmund summoned the butler to bring a decanter and two glasses. He continued pacing in silence until it was delivered. He poured each of them a glass, then sat down behind his desk and gestured for Max to be seated in a chair across from him.

"Before my wife died," he began without preamble, "we were a large, boisterous family. Our eldest child, Rosie, was the liveliest of the lot. Her little face always wreathed in smiles, constantly into some kind of mischief. I confess that when Louisa died, I became so wrapped up in my own grief that I did not notice the change in Rosie. I daresay it was harder on her than anyone, because she was the oldest, just fourteen, and had to take charge of the rest of her brothers and sisters. A huge responsibility, especially when I did nothing to help her."

He paused and seemed lost in some distant memory, his glass poised halfway to his mouth and his gaze somewhere beyond Max's shoulder. Max waited in silence, and a moment later Sir Edmund continued his narrative.

"It became easy to let Rosie take care of this and take care of that, until finally she had complete charge of the house, all the duties once performed by her mother. We took all of her time away so that she had no life of her own." A note of profound regret crept into his voice. "I have only just realized all this, since she went away to London. I allowed the fire to die in that lively young girl."

"It did not die," Max said. "It was merely smoldering beneath the surface. It flared to life again in London, I assure you."

"So I have been told." He took a deep swallow of wine and then continued. "But once she realized her foolish mistake about dying, she doused that fire with a vengeance. She won't speak of what happened in London—though her siblings are pressing hard to know all the scandalous details. She is pretending it never happened. Or, as she told you, is pretending it happened to someone else, someone who doesn't exist."

"She is afraid to admit that she is that person, the spirited Miss Lacey who set London on its ears."

"Yes, I believe you've got it right. It is much easier for her to be plain old Rosie, to slip back into the life of convention and responsibility. That other person—"

"Rosalind."

"—frightens her. To think that she might be capable of losing control, of flying in the face of propriety, of shirking her responsibilities, scares her. Dammit all, I wish it hadn't taken all this drama to make me see what was happening to Rosie. I tell you what, Davenant."

"Yes?"

"I will help you."

Max threw back his head and allowed a wave of relief to wash over him. If Sir Edmund would only talk to her, make her understand some of the things he had just said to Max, perhaps she would reconsider his offer.

"Frankly, I cannot believe I am saying this," Sir Edmund said, "considering your reputation. But I have a suspicion you are precisely the sort of man Rosie needs. I want her to be happy. I owe her nothing less. And I want my lively little girl back. And something tells me you could do it."

"I certainly want to try," Max said. "I am convinced the woman I knew in London is real, is lurking beneath the prim, country Rosie, just waiting to be set free again."

"I think so, too, Davenant. Now, if only I can convince Rosie. I daresay she is not quite ready to see you again just yet, after your unsuccessful meeting earlier."

"No, I do not believe that would do any good. She heard all my arguments. I think she needs to hear them from you now. I will return to the King's Head. You can send word to me there after you've had a chance to speak with her. And Sir Edmund, please tell her that I do love her."

*   *   *

"Are you certain, my dear?"

"Quite certain, Papa. I cannot marry him." Lord, how she wished this day would end, that Max would go away, and everyone would leave her alone. None of them understood. She could never be the woman Max wanted, and would grow miserable in the trying. In the end, he would learn to hate her for disappointing him. She could not bear that. She would rather not have him at all, even if it meant her heart would be forever broken.

"He's a good man, Rosie, even if he is a rake. Can you believe I am saying such a thing?" He was trying to coax a smile out of her, but she had none to give just now. "Who would ever have guessed that I would recommend a rake to my own daughter. But I like him. Have you never heard that old saw about reformed rakes making the best husbands? He loves you, Rosie. I do not believe he would ever hurt you."

Not deliberately, perhaps, but the scorn in his eyes would be pain enough. "We live in different worlds, Papa. It would not be a comfortable match."

"It is important to you to be comfortable, is it not? You would rather remain with the familiar than strike out in new directions."

"It is my decision, Papa. And I think it excessively unfair of you to expect me, after all this time, to become something other than what you have always wanted me to be, depended on me to be. I do not deserve your mockery for preferring to be comfortable. Now, if you will excuse me, I have much to do."

Rosie left the library with as much calm dignity as she could muster. When she reached her bedchamber, she closed the door and locked it, then threw herself upon the bed and wept for her broken heart.

*   *   *

"This is as sorry a business as I've ever seen," Fanny said. "How on earth did things manage to turn out so badly?"

Fanny sat on her favorite settee in the drawing room, clasping the hand of Lord Eldridge, who was doing his best to comfort her. But Fanny was as distraught as she could be, after receiving another disturbing letter from Edmund and a difficult visit from Max.

"How is he taking it?" Lord Eldridge asked.

"Max? Not well, as you can imagine. He really did love the girl. But like all men—forgive me, me dear, but it's true—he takes solace in anger. He paced and growled like a caged bear, spitting out horrid venom about her stubbornness, her groundless fears and anxieties, her lack of backbone."

"You know, Fanny, this may be for the best in the long run. If that's how Max sees her, then she may have been right to refuse him."

"I cannot agree with you, Jonathan. She is making a terrible mistake. How she can toss away the love of a man like that is beyond me. Especially when I know she loves him, too. Did you not see it every time she looked at him?"

"I did, indeed. I confess I thought they seemed well suited."

"So did I!" Fanny's voice rose on a note of desperation. "Oh, Jonathan, I cannot simply sit by and watch two lives be ruined. What should I do?"

"Not much you can do with Max here and Rosalind in Devon. They must meet again if they are ever to solve their difficulties."

"And Max is unlikely ever to want to show his face at Wycombe again any time soon. If ever."

"So, Rosalind must come to London."

Fanny gave Lord Eldridge an incredulous look. "Nothing will persuade that girl to come back here.

According to both Edmund and Max, she is so mortified she has crawled into a sort of shell, trying to pretend none of it ever happened."

"Know what I think?" Lord Eldridge said. "I think all this mortification we keep hearing about has nothing to do with any stunt she pulled while in town. I'll wager she's more embarrassed that she believed she was going to die, that people will ridicule her foolishness."

Fanny's eyes widened at the man's unexpected perspicacity. "You may be right, Jonathan. But outside of you and Max, I've told no one. She would not have to be afraid of any sort of public humiliation, if only we could contrive to get her back in town. I cannot, though, imagine what would convince her to come."

"What if you fell ill?"

"Don't be silly, darling," she said while patting his hand, "you know I am fit as a draft horse."

"But what if Rosalind *believed* you to be ill?" he said. "She developed quite a deep affection for you, my dear. Do you not think she would feel obliged to rush to your side if you asked her?"

"Jonathan, you clever man, I think you've hit on just the thing." She reached over and kissed his cheek.

"I do not believe Fanny would joke about something like this," Sir Edmund said.

"She really is ill?" Rosie asked.

"Here, read her letter and judge for yourself." Sir Edmund passed the parchment to Rosie and hoped she would be convinced by Fanny's words. She wrote that she had grown terribly ill, had seen Sir Nigel Leighton, and been told to remain in bed indefinitely. She wondered if Edmund would be so obliging as to send Rosie to Berkley Square to lend her companionship until Fanny had recovered her strength.

Sir Edmund would not reveal to Rosie that a second sheet had been enclosed, one for his eyes only, in which Fanny spelled out her plan to get Max and Rosalind back together. For once in his life, Sir Edmund was in total agreement with his sister.

"She is a bit vague about the nature of her illness," Rosie said. "What do you suppose is wrong?"

"I do not know for sure, of course, but Fanny has occasionally been troubled by a weak heart."

"Fanny?"

Sir Edmund realized how unlikely a notion that was the moment he said it. "Yes, but it could be something else." He stood before Rosie and took both her hands in his. "My dear, you know I was not thrilled to have you stay with my infamous sister when you went to London, but I had no proper reason to deny you the visit. Fanny wrote to me several times while you were in town, praising you to the moon, thanking me for allowing you to visit, and so on. She became quite fond of you, Rosie."

"And I of her," Rosie said. "She is the most remarkable woman, Papa. Getting to know Fanny is the one part of my trip I do not regret. I hope you are not offended, Papa, but I absolutely adore her."

"Then you should go to her, my dear," he said, squeezing her hands and signaling he was not offended by her admiration for Fanny. "She is not a young woman, you know. She realizes you might be uneasy returning to London after all that has happened, but you can see that she says she will have to keep you quietly to herself since she is confined to bed. No one need know you've come back to London. And even if they do, no one but Fanny and Lord Eldridge—and Davenant—know why you returned home. As for Davenant," he said, and Rosie braced herself for another attempt to change her mind about Max, "he mentioned something about an estate in Suffolk. In fact, most of the *ton* has returned to their various country homes. London will be very thin of company. There should be no embarrassment of any kind, if that is what concerns you."

"I daresay you are right, Papa."

"Fanny needs you, my dear."

"Then I must go to her."

Chapter 16

"All things considered, Max darling, you cannot deny it was an eventful Season."

Max raised a sardonic brow. "Eventful is not the term I would have chosen," he said.

"But you must admit you were not bored. I recall sitting here with you before the start of the Season, listening to your complaints of constant tedium, of how the whole social whirl of the Season had begun to bore you to death."

"It was more true than you know." Max still carried Freddie Moresby's note, though he no longer regarded his friend's option as one he would ever consider for himself, even in the wake of Rosalind's rejection. That was one thing he retained from the London Rosalind: a respect for life. Max found it ironic that he had learned the lesson better than the teacher.

"And I was worried about my tedious niece," Fanny said. "How wrong we both were."

"Fanny, you know I adore you, but I am going to have to cease visiting if you insist on always bringing her up in the conversation. It was a painful interlude, but I wish to forget and move on. Can we not speak of something else?"

"Yes, of course, my boy. Did you hear—"

She was interrupted by the drawing room doors opening and the entrance of Rosalind.

Rosalind?

"Rosalind!" Fanny shrieked. She leapt to her feet, let out a mournful moan, and collapsed in a heap on the settee.

Max did not know what startled him more, the sudden appearance of Rosalind or Fanny's uncharacteristic and overly dramatic swoon.

Rosalind, avoiding Max's eye, rushed to her aunt's side. "Aunt Fanny!" She stroked the flushed cheek and patted the limp hand. "What is she doing out of bed?"

Max felt confused, as though he'd wandered into some sort of stage farce and didn't know his lines. "I beg your pardon?"

"She is not supposed to leave her bed, poor thing, though I cannot imagine Fanny obeying such an order."

What the devil? Was Fanny ill? He bent over the prone figure of his dear friend and touched a hand to her bright silver hair.

"Let us do what we can to revive her. Max, do you have a handkerchief?"

"Yes, of course." He absently tugged at his waistcoat pocket, retrieved the handkerchief, and handed it out to Rosalind, his eyes never leaving Fanny. If she was ill, why had she not told him?

"You dropped something, Max."

"What?"

"Never mind. Here, I have dampened the cloth with a bit of water from the drinks tray. Perhaps we can cool her face with it." Rosalind knelt beside Max and dabbed at Fanny's brow with the cool, wet cloth.

Fanny's eyes fluttered and she gave a shuddery moan that bordered on a wail. Max studied her with growing suspicion.

"Aunt Fanny, are you able to sit up?" Rosalind asked. "Are you feeling any better?"

"Rosalind? Is that you?"

Fanny's voice was so thin and pitiful, Max had to

turn away or burst out laughing. What a performance! Worthy of Mrs. Siddons. Max would have to scold her later for giving him such a scare. He knew exactly what she was up to now, and by Jove, it had worked.

Rosalind was here.

No longer concerned for his crafty old friend, Max was able to stand back and enjoy the sight of Rosalind. Rosie. Whoever the hell she was. She looked like Rosalind to him, fashionably dressed in a pelisse of green striped sarsnet and a Parisian bonnet trimmed on the edges in the same fabric. An improvement over the shapeless brown sack she'd been wearing at Wycombe.

She fussed with Fanny, who gave her niece a great deal of trouble as she was being lifted to a sitting position, groaning all the while. Rosalind's brow was furrowed in concern and she arranged a cushion at Fanny's back.

"You had better call Stokes," Fanny said in a strained little whine. "She can help me to my room. But please hurry. I feel so weak."

Careful Fanny. Doing it a bit too strong.

"Of course, aunt. I will go get Stokes myself. You just sit quietly. Max will look after you." She rose to her feet in a single fluid movement that reminded Max of other more sensual movements he'd witnessed. He became aware of a tightness in his groin.

When Rosalind had gone, Max closed the doors and turned to Fanny. "One more mournful moan, my dear, and you will give yourself away."

Fanny opened one eye and her lips began to twitch. "Hush, boy. I got her here. The rest is up to you. Don't botch it this time."

Max leaned down to kiss her flushed and very healthy cheek. "Thank you, my dear. I will do my best. I hope Stokes is in on the game?"

Before he could say more, Rosalind and Stokes, Fanny's maid, came bustling into the room. Max stepped aside to allow them to fret and fuss over Fanny. Stokes, obviously in Fanny's confidence regarding this charade, took charge and directed the complicated operation of getting Fanny to her feet. With Rosalind under one arm and Stokes under the other, they managed to propel Fanny toward the door.

"I'll take her from here, miss," Stokes said. "When she has one of these spells, she don't like anyone but me around her. I know what to do. You just wait down here until I get her settled in bed."

"Are you certain I can't help?" Rosalind asked.

"There's no need," Stokes said.

"Thank you, Rosalind," Fanny said in a weak voice. "I am so pleased you are here. Come up later and see me."

With Fanny leaning heavily on Stokes, the two women made their slow progress up the stairs.

Max gestured for Rosalind to join him in the drawing room. With concerned glances over her shoulder, she kept an eye on Fanny until she was out of sight beyond the landing. It was only then that she was able to concentrate her attention on Max. He noted a slight flush to her cheeks as she entered the room and took a seat.

"I am surprised to see you, Rosalind."

"I daresay you are."

"What brings you back to town? Fanny's illness?"

"Yes, of course. I came as soon as I heard. But, Max, what exactly is wrong with her, do you know? She was not ill when I left."

"I believe it is to do with her lungs," he extemporized. "Limited wind, or some such thing."

"Oh. Papa thought it might be her heart again."

"Well, um, the heart may be involved in it, too. The heart and the lungs. That Leighton fellow keeps a tight lip. Never know for sure unless he tells you right out, which he won't since I'm no relation to Fanny."

"Then perhaps he will tell me. I hope so. I'm so concerned for her."

"It is good to see you, Rosalind. Are you well?"

"Yes, thank you."

"And your family, your father?"

"Very well, thank you."

"You must be sure to give the twins my regrets for not staying long enough to teach them to tie the oriental."

"They were . . . disappointed."

"Well. It was best that I left, under the circumstances."

"Yes. I'm sorry, Max."

He shrugged. "I am trying to live with it."

"This is very awkward," she said. "Perhaps I should just go upstairs and see to Fanny." She rose and moved toward the doors.

"No!" Fanny would have his head if Rosalind came upstairs too soon, before she was laid out like the proper invalid. "Stokes will let you know when you can see her. Look, if it makes you uncomfortable to have me here, I shall take my leave. Do you suppose we could have a talk, you and me, before you go back to Devon?"

"Perhaps."

"Perhaps. Well, that is something, anyway. Goodbye, Rosalind. Rosie."

When she heard the front door close, Rosie let out her breath with a whoosh. This was going to be difficult. With Fanny's peculiar illness and Max's unnerving proximity, she did not know how she would manage.

To keep her mind on something besides Max and those deep brown eyes, she rang for a footman and set about settling in again. Her bandboxes had already been placed in the bedchamber she'd used before. It was almost as though she'd never left.

Violet was busy arranging clothes in the wardrobe when Rosie entered. "Oh, miss. You ain't even taken off your spencer and hat."

"Oh." She'd been so distracted, first by Fanny and then by Max, she had not even recalled she was still wearing her traveling gear. "How silly of me. Here, take this bonnet, Violet. And I'll just—hold on, what's this?" Something crinkled in the pocket of her skirt. "Oh." It was the paper that had dropped from Max's waistcoat when he pulled out his handkerchief. Rosie had stuffed it in her own pocket and, in the urgency of the moment, forgot about it.

It would make for a good excuse to see him again, though she knew that was a bad idea. Rosie was about to lay the paper down on her dressing table, when she noticed a great scrawling M at the bottom of the sheet. She'd never before seen Max's handwriting that she could recall, but she was not surprised to discover he wrote his initial with a flourish.

She wondered what the note was. It was a small sheet, not a standard size, and folded in half. Why would he be keeping a note from himself? It was none of her business. She put the paper on the table, determined not to succumb to curiosity.

But that big M kept winking at her. Good heavens, it was just a little note, probably nothing of any importance. What harm would it do to have a little peek? Before her conscience could interfere, Rosie picked up the note and unfolded it. It took only an instant to scan the words, and another for the cry to escape her lips.

> Life is a bore.
> I no longer have a reason to stay alive.
> So I won't. Good-bye world.
> —M

No! Please God, no. He had said he had been planning to commit suicide, but she hadn't believed him.
He said she made him want to live again. But then
she rejected him. Did he no longer want to live because she turned him down? Oh God, had she brought
him to this?

"Miss? Miss? What is it?" Violet was staring at her
wild-eyed.

"I have to go," Rosie said absently. "I have to go."

She made her way down the stairs and out the
front door before she became muddled. She'd only
been there once and it was dark. Where was his house?

She couldn't think. Her mind was in a whirl. If
Max was going to kill himself, it was all her fault. She
couldn't bear it. Oh God, she couldn't bear it.

Where was his house?

Mount Street. She remembered him saying it as
they stood outside the hackney. *We're on Mount Street,
just a few steps from Berkley Square.* But which way?
She looked around frantically. Lansdown House stood
at the bottom of the square, so she headed in the opposite direction and soon ran into the junction of
Davies and Mount streets.

She practically ran up Mount Street, but could not
recall the number, or any detail of the outside of the
house. She hadn't been paying attention. She hadn't
taken her eyes off Max.

She could not make herself believe that the man
who'd made such sweet love to her was going to end
his life. Had she hurt him that badly? Had he loved
her that much? Was he going to kill himself all because she rejected him? No, it could not be true. Please,
God, make it not true. If only she hadn't been so bloody
stubborn, so unwilling to believe that he might really
love *her* and not some phantom. If only she hadn't
been so afraid of losing him that she wouldn't allow
herself to take him. If only . . . if only . . .

She had to find his house, but not a single one looked familiar. She stopped a gentleman walking by and asked if he knew which number was Mr. Davenant's house. He did not know, and gave her a scornful look for asking such a thing.

Finally, she simply went up the steps of a random house and rang the bell. A pretty parlor maid answered. Rosie tried to keep her voice even and not betray the anxiety—the panic—that held her body in its grip.

"I am sorry to trouble you, but I am supposed to meet my aunt at Mr. Davenant's, and I have lost the direction. I know it is near here somewhere. Can you tell me which number is his?"

"Yes, miss. That'd be Number Fifteen, two doors down."

Rosie thanked her and hurried to Max's house. "Where is Max?" she demanded the instant the butler had opened the door.

"I beg your pardon, miss," he said. "If you would like to come inside, I will see if Mr. Davenant is at home."

"No, there is no time. I know the way." And she did. She remembered quite clearly being carried up this staircase and into Max's bedchamber. She brushed by the horrified butler and dashed up the stairs.

"Miss? Miss, wait!"

But she could not wait. It might be too late.

Second door on the right. It was closed. She turned the handle and swung it open.

Max stood shirtless before a bowl of water. He held a long-handled razor to his throat.

"No, Max!"

Max had time to do no more than look up before Rosalind had flung herself upon him with the force of a charging elephant, knocked him to the ground, and batted away the razor so that it nicked his jaw before clattering to the floor.

What the devil?

He had no idea what was going on, but Rosalind was sprawled atop him in a most interesting manner. He could see his astonished butler in the doorway, and with the merest flicker of an eye, he sent the man away. And suddenly her hands were all over his face, touching him, stroking him. "I won't let you do it, Max. I don't care what I said before at Wycombe. I didn't mean it. I do love you. I love you so much it hurts and I will not let you throw your life away. I won't let you do it. I won't!"

Max grabbed onto the important parts of this speech, savoring each word, and managed to snake an arm around her waist and press her closer. But curiosity made him ask, "You won't let me do what, minx?"

"I found your note," she said, her voice shaking with emotion, "the one that said life is a bore and you no longer had a reason to live."

Freddie's note. It must have fallen out of his pocket at Fanny's.

Egad, she believes I wrote it, he thought.

"I won't let you do it," she said again, and began to rain kisses upon his face. "I won't let you. You *do* have something to live for. Live for me, Max. Live for me."

What an interesting development this was. If he told her the truth, she might just slap his face for giving her a scare and go back to saying she wouldn't marry him. On the other hand . . .

"How clever you are, my minx," he said, dabbing at his bleeding chin with one hand and massaging her waist with the other. "How clever to realize I had meant to make it look like the slip of the razor. A simple accident."

"Oh, Max!" she wailed.

He heaved a sigh. "I suppose I'll just have to try something else."

"No! Max, no. You cannot do it. Live for me. Please, live for me."

"You tempt me, minx. But I don't know. If you are truly asking me to live for you, I need some reassurance. I need something permanent."

"I'll do anything. Just don't die."

"I don't think I could be satisfied with less than marriage. If I am to live for you, it will have to be as your husband. Otherwise, I might be provoked into trying again."

"I'll marry you, Max."

"Almost, you persuade me, minx. But I am not quite convinced."

She kissed him. "I will marry you. I will."

"And you promise that you really do love me? That it is not some pretense just to keep me from taking my life?"

"I do love you, Max. I do."

"Prove it."

She kissed him deeply and he wrapped both arms around her and rolled them both over so that she was pinned beneath him. Max began to pluck at her clothes.

"Prove it."

Rosie curled up beside him and rested her head on his chest. She expelled a great sigh of pure satisfaction. It had been every bit as good as the first time. Better, even.

Max's fingers began to stroke her hair and she purred like a kitten. "I'm holding you to all those promises, minx. You're going to love me and you're going to marry me."

"Yes, Max."

"Before you can disappear again, I am sending in an announcement to the papers. Tomorrow."

"Max?"

"Hm?"

"What about my reputation? I'm still the Scarlet Woman in those prints. After everything I've done, I suspect I will not be received everywhere."

"Nonsense, my love. We will be the most popular couple in town. Everyone will want to see the infamous rake and his scarlet woman. I daresay the *ton* will find it all quite romantic."

"And so it is."

"And so it is."

"I'm ever so glad you didn't go through with it, Max. I would have died if you had died."

Max rolled over and kissed her. "Remind me one day to tell you about my friend Freddie Moresby."

"Later."

"Much later."

Epilogue

The quiet village of Upper Wycombe had not seen such excitement since lightning struck the steeple of St. Michael's back in '83. Never, in recent memory, had its ranks been swollen by as many swells and noblemen as now gathered for the wedding of Miss Lacey of Wycombe Hall.

The bride was herself somewhat abashed at the upheaval caused by the arrival of so many guests. Though for a short time she had been the center of attention in London, she had never been so in her own neighborhood, and it was disconcerting at best.

The stress had not let up since her sister Ursula, Lady Walgrave, had confronted Rosie upon her return from town. "It is not enough," she had complained, "that you embarrassed the family beyond repair by your unseemly behavior. But now you must marry that . . . that libertine. The man is notorious. Lord, Rosie, you are as bad as our aunt. How shall I ever hold my head up in Society again?"

Papa had been delighted with the outcome of his and Fanny's machinations. After so many years of estrangement, Rosie hoped to see a renewed affection between them. She had scolded her aunt for frightening her with feigned illness, and she extracted a promise that Fanny would come to Wycombe Hall for the wedding. Papa had gladly seconded the invitation.

Fanny had arrived two days before the wedding, in the company of Lord Eldridge and the bridegroom. The entire family had been on hand to greet the arrivals, including both Pamela and Ursula and their husbands. Max was on the spot with a very long and very satisfactory greeting, not giving Rosie the chance to object to so public a display. Ursula's gasp only incited him to prolong the kiss. When he finally pulled away, he announced to all assembled that he had happy news to report.

He tugged Fanny forward by the elbow, her bright primrose sarsnet dress and dashing Calendonia cap catching the morning sun. "I am pleased," Max said, "to introduce newlyweds Lord and Lady Eldridge, married just three days."

"Aunt Fanny!" Rosie threw her arms around her aunt and kissed her cheek. "What a wonderful surprise. Why didn't you tell me?"

Fanny looked to her beaming husband and smiled. "All this talk of weddings got me to feeling sentimental, I suppose. Jonathan's been asking for years, and I finally decided to take the plunge. And let me tell you, my girl, it is a most pleasurable state, even at my age. I highly recommend it to you."

After further congratulations, including an unexpected hug from Sir Edmund, and introductions to the gathered guests, Fanny tugged Rosie inside and eventually managed to arrange a moment of privacy with her niece.

"I expect Max will be pleased to see his family," Fanny said as she accepted a cup of tea from Rosie.

"He will, if the twins give him any peace. It is their life's ambition to return to school with the most artistically arranged cravats ever seen at Harrow. They have been waiting rather impatiently for arrival of the Master of Neckcloths. I hope they allow poor Max five minutes alone with his family."

"Have they all arrived?"

"Indeed," Rosie said. "The earl and countess are here, as is Lady Gresham, Max's sister, though her husband, the marquess, is out of the country on business. And Colonel Davenant and his wife are here as well. Ursula has been quite beside herself to be in such elevated company. She has undergone a complete change of heart and decided that my marrying Max is not such a bad thing after all, since it brings an earl and a marchioness into her circle."

"Hmph. As if they would have anything to do with the foolish girl. How are you holding up, my dear?"

"To be perfectly honest," Rosie said, "I just wish it was over and Max and I could get on with our lives. Such a lot of fuss and bother!"

"Why don't you escape?"

"What do you mean?"

"You have the license. You and Max could simply dash off and get yourselves married somewhere else and leave the rest of us to our own devices."

Rosie lifted a questioning brow. "But all the planning, the guests, the parties, the—"

"So? What does it matter? It is all nothing more than an excuse for friends and family to gather together. Well, we're all here now and can enjoy ourselves just the same, with or without a wedding."

"It wouldn't be proper," Rosie said, though her mind began to whirl with possibilities.

"Confound it, girl, you sound just like that blasted sister of yours. You never cared for what was proper when you were in London."

"I know, but—"

"And what did it get you? A lifetime of solitary repentance? No, it won you a perfectly marvelous man every woman in town has been angling after for years. If you had not thrown propriety to the winds, he might never have given you a second glance. Now that you've got him, what the devil does it matter if you do the thing by the book? Why not just do as you please?"

Rosie gave a wistful sigh. "Oh, I should dearly love to escape all the hubbub and just be alone with Max."

"What's stopping you?"

Nothing at all, as it turned out. Less than an hour later, she smuggled a small bandbox into the boot of the curricle she'd borrowed from Thomas and coaxed Max into taking a brief drive.

"What's all this, minx?" he said. "Anxious to display your driving skills on an uncrowded country road?"

"I just felt like a bit of kidnapping."

"Egad, are you stealing me away? How delightful." He snaked his arm around her and gave a provocative squeeze. "Someplace very, very private, I hope."

"Not too private. We will need witnesses, I believe."

His head jerked up from nuzzling her neck. "Witnesses? What the devil are you up to, minx?"

"We're eloping, Max."

"What?"

"I have the license in my reticule and a bag packed for the night. We must hurry, though. It is not a special license, so we must be married before noon. I think we can make Plymtree if I really push the team."

Max gaped at her open-mouthed for a long moment before his face transformed itself into a smile. "By Jove, you are the bold miss I knew in London after all. I knew it. I told you it could not have all been pretense. You really are a minx." He tilted her face toward him and kissed her.

"Stop it, Max! We'll never make it by noon if you distract me."

"Forgive me, minx. I am your captive. Drive on."

Less than a week later, a new print by Mr. Row-landson was displayed prominently in every print shop in London. Entitled "The Matrimonial Race, or

The Bride Gets her Man," it showed a sleek sporting vehicle with a dashing young woman at the ribbons, dressed all in red, and a terror-struck man at her side, hanging on for his life, his leg shackled to hers. Below it was written:

> When Mr. D—— offered for Miss L——
> 'Twas a thing so great and rare
> She drove top speed to the nearest church
> To marry him then and there.
>
> Such brash behavior goes to show:
> When seeking wedded bliss
> The newly married Mrs. D——
> Was no milk and water miss.